KEENE'S LIBERTY

KEENE'S LIBERTY

Book Three of
Keene's Revolution

*The Story of an English Spy in
the War against France*

Derek Wilson

severn House

This first world edition published in Great Britain 2002 by
SEVERN HOUSE PUBLISHERS LTD of
9–15 High Street, Sutton, Surrey SM1 1DF.
This first world edition published in the USA 2002 by
SEVERN HOUSE PUBLISHERS INC of
595 Madison Avenue, New York, N.Y. 10022.

British Library Cataloguing in Publication Data

Wilson, Derek, 1935–
  Keene's liberty
  1. Keene, George (Fictitious character) – Fiction
  2. Espionage, British – History – 18th century – Fiction
  3. France – History – Revolution, 1789–1799 – Fiction
  4. Historical fiction
  I. Title
  823.9'14 [F]

ISBN 0-7278-5642-1

Typeset by Palimpsest Book Production Ltd.,
Polmont, Stirlingshire, Scotland.
Printed and bound in Great Britain by
MPG Books Ltd., Bodmin, Cornwall.

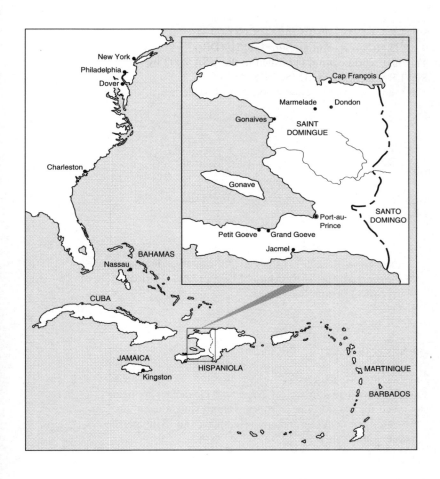

Prologue

Gunboat Diplomacy – 19 May 1793

The weather was fine. The sun, as yet imparting little warmth, traced a shimmering path across the eastward ocean and to the west the coastline of South Carolina ridged the horizon as the morning mist dispersed. An onshore breeze encouraged the slave ship *Christabel* towards her port of call and all hands were eager to savour the delights of Charleston.

But it was Sunday.

On Sundays, barring emergencies, all work on board the *Christabel* stopped for three morning hours. Sunday was the Lord's day and Samuel Thorpe, shipmaster, was the Lord's man, ever since an evening in Bristol thirty years before when, with a gut full of porter, he had staggered out of the rain into a meeting hall and encountered a new kind of intoxicant issuing from the lips of John Wesley. Since then he had considered conversion of his crews a prime objective of his maritime activity. That was why Sunday forenoons were given over to the lusty singing of hymns and an hour-long sermon delivered by the master, followed by a period of silence, during which the ship's complement were encouraged to meditate on 'the works of the Lord and his wonders in the deep'.

So, on this spring sabbath, divine service being over, Thorpe's men lounged about the deck and cast longing eyes towards the American coast, while their vessel rode easily at anchor, her sails neatly furled. From time to time,

1

other ships passed the *Christabel*, on their way in or out of port. Some hailed her to know if she needed assistance but hastened about their business after being challenged by Thorpe through his speaking trumpet to 'honour the Lord's day'.

The sea approaches to Charleston were busy with traffic. The magnificent harbour was a gateway to a plantation economy rich in rice and cotton and its merchants were as eager to trade its bounty with the Old World as their counterparts in London, Bordeaux, Lisbon and Amsterdam were to do business with this thriving entrepôt of the young United States of America. No one aboard the *Christabel*, therefore, paid particular attention to the frigate sailing under the republic's colours which appeared on the starboard quarter and rapidly closed on the English vessel.

Only when the American ship took in sail and was obviously intent on coming alongside did the mate feel any concern. 'Ware as ye go, *Buscadee*!' he bellowed, misreading the name painted along the frigate's bow. At the same time he sent a boy to rouse the master.

Thorpe sat at his cabin table crouched over a large Bible and glared up at the messenger, his thick eyebrows meeting in a deep frown. 'What is it?'

The emissary, a thirteen-year-old scrap of a lad with fire-red hair, stood close to the open door, ready to run if 'Parson' Thorpe flew into one of his customary rages. 'Mr Grinley's compliments, sir, and would you be pleased to come on deck on account there's a Yankee warship sniffing around us.'

'Let 'im sniff!' The master waved the boy away. 'We ain't got nothing to hide.' He lowered his eyes to the heavy black print of the book of Numbers.

The boy had scarcely made his thankful exit when Thorpe's concentration was broken again. There were shouts and the thud of running feet on the deck above his head. With a muted oath, he hauled himself to his feet and lumbered from the cabin.

The scene that confronted him on deck was so confused and unexpected that it took him several moments to understand it. There were strangers swarming over his ship. Armed strangers. Some of them were holding groups of his crew at swordpoint. He took two strides into the melée. That was as far as he got. His arms were grabbed from behind by two pistol-brandishing sailors from the ship that he could now see standing alongside the *Christabel*.

The marauders hustled him up the companionway to his own poop deck. There, at the rail, surveying the brawl which was all but over, stood a tall young man in the blue coat and bicorn of a naval captain but with a tricoloured sash around his waist. Languidly he turned to face Thorpe.

'You're the master of this vessel?' he asked.

Thorpe spluttered almost incoherently. 'What's the meaning of this outrage—'

'Your name, sir?' The American was infuriatingly calm, in full control of the situation.

'Samuel Thorpe.' The master glowered. 'And what son of Beelzebub dares to board an honest merchantman in the home waters of a friendly nation?'

The young man threw back his head and laughed. 'Son of Beelzebub? Yes, I like that.' He swept off his hat in an elaborate bow. 'Jeremiah Bowen, captain of the US privateer *Embuscade*, at your service, sir.'

Thorpe stared back. He was trembling with rage at the arrogance of this sneering interloper and struggled to find words. 'Privateer? Common pirate, more like! Since when did the American government sanction attacks on British ships engaged in legitimate trade with their country?'

Bowen scratched his head theatrically before replacing the bicorn. 'Ah, now, that's a political question and I ain't no politician. But as to legitimate trade, well now, let me see. Would I be right in thinking that the *Christabel*'s cargo is slaves?'

'What's my cargo got to do with it?'

'Just that our Revolutionary brothers in France don't take kindly to slavery.'

Thorpe was bewildered. 'To the devil with the Frogs. Your government in Philadelphia hasn't been so insane as to follow French ways.'

The last trace of humour drained from Bowen's pinched features. His reply had the ring of religious conviction. 'The republic is the people and the people believe in liberty for all. Politicians only exist to represent the will of the people. That's true in France. It's true here. Soon it will be true in Britain and the rest of the world. Mr Thorpe, your ship is commandeered in the name of the people.' The captain glanced at the sailors who were still restraining the Englishman. 'Escort the master to his cabin.'

'I'll see you swing for this!' Thorpe roared as he was forced back to the companionway. But the captain of *Embuscade* was already calling for sails to be set and anchor weighed. He gave no sign of having heard the imprecation.

GENET

'A young gentleman . . . enamoured to
distraction with republican liberty.'

John Adams

One

G eorge Keene looked around the brightly lit ballroom
and wondered why he had not made the move to
America a long time ago. The scene lacked the high-polished
elegance he had witnessed in other capitals. The state rooms
of imperial Vienna dwarfed the reception apartments of
the Randolph mansion. The houses of the haut monde
in pre-Revolutionary Paris were more a-glitter with tall
mirrors and elaborate chandeliers. The company in London
exceeded that before him in variety and sheer style. Yet
there was a relaxed gaiety about the men and women who
negotiated the intricacies of the gavottes and minuets trilled
out by a German band that distracted attention from the
fact that their fashions had been discarded in Europe a full
twelvemonth since. Having indulged himself in the dancing
for an hour or more, Keene was content, for the moment,
simply to be glad to be here; to stand in one corner of the
crowded chamber, sipping a cool glass of lemonade and
watching the swirling scene.

And to be watched. Since his arrival in Philadelphia a
week before, the tall, fair-haired Englishman had been
the object of considerable curiosity and attention. He had
appeared on the Delaware quayside among a dozen passengers disembarked from a fast merchantman, a well-dressed,
quiet-spoken young man of some thirty summers. He came
unannounced, unexpected and unaccompanied. Those curious enough to make enquiry of his fellow passengers learned
only that he was single, that he came from London and that
he was visiting relatives at Germanstown, Pennsylvania.

If George had hoped to slip discreetly into the newly independent nation, putting his turbulent past behind him, he reckoned without the concerns and inquisitiveness that stalked the coffee houses and salons of Philadelphia. This was a small community, self-confident, welcoming, conscious of forging a new identity for itself. Yet it also looked with mingled fascination, contempt and anxiety at the Old World whose political shackles it had cast off but whose emotional and cultural bonds it could not untie. The United States of America had been a new planet in the solar system of nations for ten years, and ten years was not long enough to convince the deep-rooted kingdoms and republics of Europe that its independence was a fait accompli for all time.

'States they may be; united they most certainly ain't.' That verdict, recently proclaimed in the British House of Lords, was accepted by many among the political class of the Old World – and, reluctantly, by not a few in that of the New. Each of the thirteen free territories perched on the edge of a vast unknown continent, shared with French, Spanish and British colonists as well as hundreds of indigenous tribes, was still sorting out its own constitution as well as its relationship to the federal government. Each was still rent by the same divisions of class, race and religion that its citizens and their ancestors had once fled from. The hope indulged by George III that his rebellious subjects might yet be forced by harsh reality to return to the fold was by no means universally dismissed as a pipe dream.

Any visitor from his Majesty's realm was, therefore, scrutinised by the unofficial inquisition of society gossips. The lack of any known facts about George Keene was a vacuum readily filled by conjecture. He was, it was confidently rumoured, a handsome ne'er-do-well on the run from creditors or from the vengeful relatives of some unfortunate maid to whom he had pledged marriage. More sinister tongues asserted with equal conviction that the reticent Englishman was a spy sent by William Pitt to sow dissension and to gather information about the activities of the federal government in Philadelphia.

The latter suspicion was, at one and the same time, close to and far from the truth. Keene had until only a few weeks before been a member of the British intelligence service operated on behalf of the Prime Minister, Pitt, by his master intriguer, Sir Thomas Challoner. In the space of a few months he had completed two extremely hazardous missions in France, missions which had come within an ace of costing him his life on several occasions. It was work for which he had little stomach and from which he had determined at the earliest opportunity to escape.

'Escape' was the operative word. He knew that Challoner would never allow one of his best operatives to 'retire'. Good agents were hard to come by and expensive to train and Pitt was committed to the espionage war with the leaders of Revolutionary France. He remained convinced that the only way to stop Maximilien Robespierre and his Committee of Public Safety tightening their grip on the land of the late Louis XVI and spreading further abroad the contagion of their socially destructive ideas was to undermine it from within by covert activity; by sending money and spies to help and encourage those elements in France which were opposed to the new order. But that order, after more than four years of bloody conflict, seemed no nearer to being toppled than it had when the Paris mob had stormed the Bastille or cheered the public execution of their king. Keene had no idea what the outcome of the Revolution would be. He was not even sure in his own mind that he wanted it to fail if that meant the restoration of a vengeful royalist government. The one thing that he was clear about was that his part in the conflict was over.

So he had 'escaped'. He had slipped out of London at the first opportunity, travelled incognito to Bristol and bought himself a berth on the first America-bound ship. Beyond regaining his freedom and striking a blow at Challoner in return for all the trials and humiliations he had cynically heaped on his unwilling agent, Keene had no plans beyond calling on maternal relatives in Pennsylvania whom he had never met in the hope that they might be able to provide him with useful contacts which would lead to employment – any employment. There must, he had reasoned, be many openings for young men of education and talent, men as ready to turn their backs on the past and embrace the future as was the new nation itself.

'George, you're looking horribly solemn. Aren't you enjoying yourself?'

Keene turned with a smile to the dark-haired, diminutive figure of Maria Oakland, who came to stand beside him. There was a warmth and freshness about her which seemed to symbolise the welcome he had received in rural Pennsylvania. His uncle's family had embraced him with enthusiasm but without fuss, as though the appearance of unknown relatives was an everyday occurrence. 'You must allow us old men a few moments rest,' he replied.

'Old? Stuff!' His cousin prodded him with her fan. 'You know you're the most eligible young man in the room. See how everyone's looking at us. All the unmarried women are devilish jealous of me for having you as my escort.'

Keene laughed. 'And you're loving it.'

'Absolutely! These Randolph balls are usually so formal and dull. People just come to see and be seen and to horse-trade their daughters. I find the company boring and the company finds me boring. But this year it's different. Everyone wants to talk to me and ask me about my handsome and mysterious English cousin. I'm having enormous fun making up outrageous stories about you.'

'I expect you're just getting to the age when young ladies start actually enjoying balls.'

Maria pouted. 'Now you *do* sound like an old man! That's just what my father says: "You're eighteen, my dear, and you really should be looking around for a suitable young man. Your mother and I won't force you, but . . ." It's a threat, of course: "Find a husband or we'll find one for you." '

10

'And husbands don't feature in your scheme of things?'

'That depends.' Maria turned her frank, blue-grey eyes upon him with a disarmingly appraising scrutiny.

Keene diverted the conversation into other channels. 'So this is the cream of Philadelphia society?' he asked, gazing across the crowded ballroom.

'Oh, yes, the Randolphs' autumn ball is one of *the* high points of the calendar. All our matrons fight tooth and nail to get invitations. Not to be invited is the first step on the slippery slope to social obscurity.'

'So, point out some of the leading Philadelphians to me.'

Maria sighed. 'Oh, very well, sobersides, but only if you fetch me a lemonade and promise me the next dance.'

Moments later, when she had a tall glass in her left hand, Maria linked her other through Keene's arm and walked him around the room's perimeter. 'Well, you were introduced to our host, Edmund Randolph, as we arrived.'

'I gather you don't much like the Attorney General.'

Maria wrinkled her nose. 'He's a Virginian.'

'That's bad?'

'Virginians think they're the only Americans, especially families like the Randolphs, who've been here for ever. Of course, you know the old man seated over there on the dais.'

Keene peered through a gap that had opened up among the dancers at the portly figure in the short, military-style wig, who sat erect on the raised platform reserved for the guest of honour and his party. 'Washington.'

Maria nodded enthusiastically. 'The great man himself.'

'Another Virginian, isn't he?'

Maria ignored the taunt. 'You see the two men standing beside the President? They're the ones who really run the government, or so father says. The taller is Alexander Hamilton and other one is Thomas Jefferson . . . They hate each other,' she added simply.

'Why?' Keene asked.

11

Derek Wilson

Maria shrugged. 'They're politicians.' To her the reason was self-evident or inconsequential or both.

They continued their perambulation, Maria pointing out with entertaining and probably slanderous appraisal the men and women who dominated the life of the capital. They were strolling past a corner where a semicircle of chairs were arranged in a recess when an effervescence of gay laughter broke from the group ensconced there. Glancing in that direction, Keene saw that the focus of attention was a man of about his own age, flamboyantly dressed, who was keeping his companions entertained with anecdotes that were obviously amusing.

Keene felt a tug at his arm and allowed himself to be drawn away. 'A popular fellow,' he observed.

'Certainly popular with himself,' Maria responded tartly, 'but you would not like him.'

'Why are you so sure?'

'You are English and M. Genet, or Citizen Genet as he prefers to be called, regards all Englishmen as the devil's brood.'

'And what is Citizen Genet's business here?'

'Officially doing whatever it is that a French chargé d'affaires is supposed to do. Unofficially, making mischief.' Maria waved the distasteful subject aside. 'Come along, George, let's dance. You promised.'

But Keene was intrigued. 'What sort of mischief?'

'Oh, all sorts – wooing every rich woman he can find who lacks the wit to see through his oily blandandering, worming his way into the homes of trusting, hospitable families, distributing cuckold horns from his knapsack. Is that list long enough for you? Now, can we *dance*?'

Keene allowed himself to be led onto the floor, wondering exactly what it was that had passed between the Frenchman and Miss Maria Oakland.

He was curious enough to raise the matter with his uncle as they rode out to inspect the stock the next morning. Jack

12

Oakland was proud of the family farm at Germanstown. What his pioneering father had begun as a very modest holding when he had settled in the colony half a century earlier had been built up into one of the largest in the region. Jack had added a butchery business to the farm and regularly drove animals into Philadelphia to be slaughtered and sold on his own premises in the town. The work kept Jack and his two sons very busy so they had largely left Maria in charge of the entertainment of her cousin.

George had enjoyed riding round the farm and the surrounding countryside with his pretty, plain-spoken young guide. It had felt like going back to his childhood in rural Norfolk. Throughout all his early years his world had been horizoned by the flat fields and spacious skyscapes of East Anglia. Then his father had grasped the opportunity to 'better' his son by securing a place for him in the household of Lord Gower. That had begun the whirlwind years of foreign travel as companion to the marquis's young heir, George Leveson-Gower. Every fresh marvel he encountered – the classical ruins of Rome and Athens, the magnificent Habsburg court of the sick and well-intentioned Joseph II, the greater, eternal majesty of the towering Alps, the mind-expanding treasures of great libraries and art collections – widened the gulf between the man and simple farm boy. Only now did Keene begin to realise what he had given up – or, rather, what had been taken from him.

'I always like to stop here for a minute or two.' Jack Oakland reined in his horse as they emerged from a belt of woodland on to a ridge which gave them a view over wide meadows to where the farmstead's buildings huddled together a couple of miles away. 'This was our boundary in my father's day,' he explained. 'Everything to the west I've added.'

Keene smiled at the burly, tanned figure beside him. Jack carried lightly his fifty or so years and his thick, black hair was only just beginning to show streaks of grey. 'You've done well,' he said.

'It hasn't always been easy, especially during the war. Germanstown was overrun by the redcoats. We were afraid we might lose everything then.' He shook his head. 'A stupid business.'

'You think the struggle for independence was a mistake?'

'Forcing us to it was a mistake. Our countries need each other. Now a bitter crop has been sown which will take generations to uproot.'

Keene looked puzzled. 'I haven't noticed any animosity. You've been very kind to me. Your neighbours and friends – they've all shown me civility.'

'Don't mistake me, George. It's a great pleasure for us to have you here and you must regard our home as yours just as long as you want. I'm afraid you won't find everyone quite so welcoming. This is a divided country and your war with France has polarised opinion here even more.' Jack urged his mare into a walk and turned her along the ridge. 'But let's not talk politics. We've got your future to sort out. Have you made any plans yet?'

'No . . . unless . . .' Keene hesitated.

'Unless what?'

'Well, I was wondering whether you could use some more help on the farm.'

Jack laughed. 'That question wouldn't have anything to do with Maria, I suppose?'

Keene shook his head. 'She's a fine young woman; a credit to you.'

'But?'

'But I don't think I'm ready for marriage yet and I'm sure there must be a great deal of competition for her hand.'

'Oh, there's certainly been no lack of interest – all one-sided, I'm afraid.'

'That Frenchman, Genet, was he one of her suitors?'

Keene's uncle frowned. 'That's a name we try not to mention here. When he arrived in Philadelphia we threw a party for him here. Several people did; natural hospitality to

14

an important visitor. He was very charming, very plausible, very man-of-the-world. He even impressed Maria – and very few men do that. He came again, a couple of times and began to pay attention to her. I'm afraid I encouraged him . . . urged Maria to welcome his advances. I was as much taken in by the scoundrel as anybody else.'

'And Maria fell for him?'

'No, I don't think so. She found him amusing and kept company with him to please me. Until she discovered the sort of man he really is.'

'How was that?'

'He arrived one day to take her riding. She was delayed for a while. When she eventually went out to the stable to find him she came across him tumbling one of the maids in the hayloft.'

'She must have been very distressed.'

'More relieved, I think. She certainly reminds me of that afternoon if ever she suspects that I'm trying to steer her in the direction of matrimony. I guess she'll chart her own course, and I know she has already become very fond of her long-lost English cousin.'

'Her long-lost and impoverished English cousin,' Keene added. 'I've absolutely nothing to offer a prospective bride.'

'Well,' Jack looked thoughtful, 'perhaps we could do something about that.'

Keene responded sharply. 'No, I'd rather you didn't!' Immediately, he realised that the words had sounded ungracious, almost surly, and the expression on his uncle's face told him that they had provoked surprise. What he could not tell his well-meaning relative was that there had been another reason for his precipitate departure from England – Thérèse. They had met and fallen in love in Paris in the early days of the Revolution. Subsequently Keene had rescued her and arranged her departure for England; hers and the child she was carrying – his child. Keene had deluded himself into imagining an idyllic future with Thérèse. But he had reckoned without the intervention of a handsome

15

young naval officer who also happened to be heir to a considerable estate.

He collected himself quickly and said, 'I'm sorry, Uncle, but I don't want you to think I was hinting at a dowry. That wasn't in my thoughts at all.'

'Nor mine, George, nor mine. This is a country in which a man has to work for his fortune. I've more respect for you than to pay you to take Maria off my hands and she wouldn't thank either of us for making such an arrangement. As to your working on the farm, that would be a waste – both for you and the country. You're a well-educated young man, widely travelled; you know how the world works. You should be in Philadelphia. We need your talents in the administration.'

'In what way?'

Jack shrugged. 'Secretary in one of the offices of state, translator, diplomatic aide. There's a real shortage of intelligent, well-qualified men to fill those sorts of posts. Last night at the ball I spoke about you with Mr Hamilton . . .'

'Alexander Hamilton?'

'Yes, the Secretary to the Treasury. He was very interested. He promised to send for you soon. You don't have to go, of course, but I think you ought to hear what he has to offer.'

Several days passed; enough for Keene to conclude that Hamilton's polite show of interest in a newly arrived Englishman was just that and no more. However, the possibility of meeting one of the nation's leaders did spur him into finding out whatever he could about the man.

His most immediate discovery was that opinion was violently divided. People either admired or loathed Alexander Hamilton. To some he was an astute politician, a man who had risen by his own efforts from being the illegitimate son of a poor immigrant woman to being President Washington's right-hand man. To others he was an arrogant and ambitious snob who sought power for its own sake. To ardent republicans Hamilton represented all that was most reactionary in the government; a politician who took Britain as his constitutional model and toadied to the country from which the United States had torn itself free. His supporters regarded the Secretary to the Treasury as a forward-looking statesman who refused to see the nation shackled by old animosities and, specifically, dissociated America from the ruinous course being pursued by France in the name of 'Liberty'.

October had turned into November, with its cutting winds from the wild interior and its dank mists rolling in from the Atlantic, before the summons came in the form of a brief letter written in a flowing hand on expensive paper sealed with Hamilton's monogram in wax. It invited – or virtually commanded – Mr George Keene to present himself at five o'clock the following day, not at the minister's office, but at his private residence.

It was raining the next afternoon as Keene, his best clothes protected by a heavy topcoat, dismounted in front of an elegant semi-mansion very much in the classical style currently favoured by America's nouveau riche. Immediately a groom rushed to collect the visitor's mount and Keene had scarcely ascended the shallow flight of steps before the large front door opened silently to admit him to a wide hall whose elegant panelling was hung with paintings by European artists. A bewigged footman in a blue coat with silver facings silently relieved Keene of his dripping outer garment and ushered him to a small withdrawing room.

The Englishman looked round at the slender mahogany furniture, the gilded mirrors and the moulded fireplace with elegant porcelain figurines arranged on the mantel. He could see why Hamilton could be accused of being too Anglophile. This room might, he realised, be replicated in any well-to-do gentleman's residence in the English shires. He was not kept waiting long. After ten minutes the flunky glided back into the room and escorted him once more across the hall.

He tapped discreetly on a door opposite and turned the brass handle.

Keene entered a long library with matching glazed bookcases arranged along each side. Hamilton was seated facing him at a writing table at the far end. He rose as Keene advanced and extended his hand. He was smaller than Keene had remembered from his distant view on the evening of the ball, and his frame was almost spare. The elegance of his apparel and the intensity of the gaze his deep-set eyes focused on his visitor reminded Keene with a shock of another politician – Maximilien Robespierre. He brushed the thought aside; there could surely be no meaningful comparison between this man and the ice-cold fanatic who held France in thrall. Yet even when the American spoke the similarity was striking. Hamilton's voice was high-pitched and what he had to say was conveyed with the minimum of precisely enunciated words. 'In the name of the President I bid you welcome to the United States of America.'

Keene found himself making a stumbled reply as he stood awkwardly facing his host across the table. But, if he was momentarily caught off guard, what happened next left him appalled and speechless.

'My other English guest you, of course, know.' Hamilton indicated a figure standing to the left of the doorway whom Keene had not noticed on his entrance.

That figure now came forward, leaning slightly on a silver-topped cane. 'Good day to you, Keene. Pleasure to see you again,' said Sir Thomas Challoner, with the faintest trace of irony in his voice.

Two

K eene was momentarily speechless and Challoner did not hesitate to fill the silence.

'Mr Hamilton and I have gone over the main details of your new assignment.' He seated himself on an upright chair with his hands before him clasped over the handle of his cane. 'This meeting is for the purpose of briefing you.'

Keene loathed the man's air of easy authority; his assumption of command. At last he found the voice to protest. 'Assignment! You have no authority . . . '

Challoner held up a hand. 'A moment, Keene.' He turned with a smile to Hamilton. 'Perhaps my associate and I might be permitted a few minutes . . . Much has happened since Mr Keene's departure from England . . . I should apprise him of the new situation.'

With a curt, 'Of course,' Hamilton rose and strode briskly from the room.

As soon as the door closed, Keene rounded on Challoner, standing before the seated figure and glowering down at him. 'You had the effrontery to follow me here!'

'Follow? Certainly not.' The older man removed his spectacles and nonchalantly polished them. '"Rendezvous" would, I think, be a more appropriate word. Certainly, that is the understanding our colonial friends – forgive me, I should say "our American friends". How difficult it is to rid one's mind of old habits . . . That is the understanding our . . . transatlantic, yes transatlantic . . . friends have of the situation.'

Keene took a couple of paces down the room. He turned.

19

'No, Sir Thomas, your smooth words won't work this time. I'm doing no more of your dirty work. You've robbed me of my good name. You've seen me branded a traitor. You've sent me ill-prepared into danger and come damned near getting me killed more than once. Well, all that's in the past. I want no more to do with you and your Machiavellian schemes. I don't know how you managed to trace me here but this is a free, independent country and you have no hold over me.'

Challoner replaced his glasses on his nose and ran a hand over his brushed-back grey hair. 'My dear Keene, you still have this distasteful tendency to reduce important matters to the purely personal. Well, if we must dwell on individual suffering, let me ask how much thought you've given to my situation. Here am I entrusted with trying to prevent, on the one hand, the spread of anarchy throughout the civilised world and, on the other, the eruption of what could be the bloodiest war Europe has ever seen. I have few, precious few, men of intelligence and resource whom I can employ in this historic – and I don't use the word lightly – this historic mission. When one of them deserts his post without warning or explanation that makes my task doubly difficult. You know full well the opposition Mr Pitt and I face in the highest circles, the constant struggle we have to obtain resources for intelligence work, the Herculean task of recruiting sufficient agents, the numerous potential sources of information where the British government needs to maintain a covert presence, the increasing guile of our adversaries. Any defection has a myriad consequences . . . '

Keene waved the arguments aside. 'How can you talk of defection? For months you've used me, manipulated me, tricked me, and all that time I've done your bidding, often against my better judgement. If you demand patriotism, haven't I given proof of it? The only reward I ask is to be allowed now to live my own life.'

'Where?' The spymaster gazed calmly at the agitated man before him.

'I beg your pardon?'

'I said, "Where?" What location do you propose in which to live out this uninhibited idyll?'

Keene searched the placid features he knew only too well, a sudden frost numbing his mind. Challoner sat smugly before him, exuding damnable confidence. Why? How could he be so sure of himself in this foreign country far away from the base of his own power?

The older man raised a quizzical eyebrow. 'Should I assume that this self-conscious new nation is the one you've chosen for your haven?'

Keene glowered. 'What point are you trying to make?'

'Merely that I'm surprised that you are unwilling to perform a simple service for your adopted country. Were I in your position I would want to impress the leaders here in Philadelphia with my devotion to their cause.' Challoner rose and began to move down the room. 'Mr Hamilton will, I expect, be disappointed to learn that you have turned down his request for aid without even hearing it. I suppose he might even decide that you are not welcome here.' He reached out a hand for the bell pull beside the fireplace.

Keene watched as Challoner tugged at the cord and informed the footman who almost instantly appeared that he was ready to resume his discussion with Mr Hamilton. What was it about this man, Keene wondered, not for the first time, that enabled him to assume command wherever he was? Whatever the secret of his authority, Keene found it profoundly irritating. He said, as the door closed, 'For God's sake, Sir Thomas, be straight with me. What's this latest scheme of yours? What can America possibly have to do with your conflict with the French? And what in Heaven's name has all this got to do with me?'

Challoner turned and stood in the middle of the room, leaning, Keene noticed for the first time, very heavily on his cane. 'To take your questions in order, my "scheme" is the same as it always has been, to try to keep a step ahead of the French and bring this ruinous Revolution of theirs to an end. How does this involve America? Well, you may be sure that I wouldn't endure an extremely disagreeable ocean crossing if it were not absolutely necessary. The simple fact is that the Jacobins in Paris are set on bringing this fledgeling nation into the war.'

'The government here won't want to involve themselves in a conflict thousands of miles away,' Keene responded with conviction.

'Don't be so sure of that.' Challoner returned to his chair and grimaced slightly as he lowered himself on to it. 'The French see it as simply calling in a debt: they helped the colonists to break away from the British crown; now it's America's turn to support her Revolutionary friends against the forces of what they call royalist tyranny and reaction. And be in no doubt, Keene, if their diplomacy succeeds it will make things devilish difficult for us.'

'Because it would cut off trade between our countries?'

'That and more. The French could use American bases to launch privateering raids against our shipping. In point of fact they've already begun to do that. They could disrupt our trade with the Indies. They could keep our navy busy in the Atlantic when it was needed in home waters. They might – Heaven forfend – set off another continental war.'

'How?'

'Linking up French settlers in Louisiana Territory with their American "allies" to wrest control from Spain and then turning their attention northwards to Canada.' He paused as Hamilton came back into the room. 'Thank you for giving us a little time, Alexander. I've been acquainting my colleague with the situation here.'

Hamilton resumed his place behind the table and waved Keene to a chair beside his other guest. 'That situation is grave, as doubtless your own enquiries have indicated.'

Keene scarcely had time to register surprise before Challoner smoothly intervened. 'It's all right, Keene, I've explained to Mr Hamilton about your arrival here incognito. He knows that as soon as word reached London about Citizen Genet's activities I naturally sent my best man by the first available ship. That inevitably meant that you left without a full briefing; hence this meeting.'

'What have you gathered about Genet, Mr Keene?' Hamilton asked.

Keene groped for a suitable comment. 'He seems to have made several enemies,' he ventured.

Hamilton nodded. 'And many friends – too many. The man is damnably plausible. He has a knack of ingratiating himself with all sorts of people, high and low. He has definitely taken in Jefferson and his Republican colleagues. But that's not the main problem; I can make sure that they don't have the President's ear. What is much more dangerous is his spreading of anarchic ideas among the people.'

Challoner hastened to fill in detail. 'Genet arrived here as chargé d'affaires six months ago and in that brief time he's been very industrious. He's travelled all along the coast from Charleston to Boston commissioning privateers to prey on British shipping. He's held public meetings to stir up pro-French sentiment. And he's founded several clandestine Jacobin clubs.'

'Surely,' Keene suggested, 'that represents an abuse of diplomatic privilege?'

'Yes, indeed,' Hamilton agreed, 'but thanks to Jefferson protecting him it took a long time to get the President to see friend Genet in his true colours. It's only in the last couple of weeks that I've been able to persuade General Washington to demand the scoundrel's recall. However, we don't know what attitude Paris will take, and even if they agree it will be several months before we can get rid of Genet. By then it may be too late.'

'America could go the same way as France.' Challoner watched carefully for the younger man's reaction.

Keene was dubious. He knew too well Sir Thomas's repertoire of persuasion.

Hamilton saw the doubt in the visitor's eyes. 'That's no

exaggeration, Mr Keene. We don't lack for rabble-rousers nor for poor immigrants made poorer still by ill fortune or their own indolence. Put those two together, add a large measure of anti-British sentiment and you have a witch's brew potent for mischief. So you see how badly we need someone with your specific skills. I speak for the President when I say how grateful we are to you for volunteering your aid so readily.'

Keene glanced at Challoner, who seemed at that moment deeply fascinated by a shelf of books to his right.

Hamilton filled the ensuing silence. 'You will report directly to me. We cannot risk using intermediaries. It scarcely needs saying that you only have to ask for whatever you need. I will do everything in my power to assist you in your mission.'

'Your mission'! The words juddered in Keene's brain and repeated themselves over and again. He paid little attention to what remained of the interview, beyond trying to appear courteous to his host. Only when he and Challoner left the house in the Englishman's closed carriage, with a servant coming on behind with his horse, did he give vent to his feelings.

'My mission! Good God, sir, you've done it again – wedged me into a corner with your damnable lies and smooth talking.'

Challoner sank back against the soft leather. 'I told our friend the plain truth: you are the best man for the job.'

'What job, exactly?'

'Despite what you've just heard, the government here are scarcely aware of how much damage a man like Genet can do. His network of Jacobin clubs is a potential threat to their whole political system but they're too naive to see it. Washington, Hamilton and the rest,' he waved a hand dismissively, 'are a bunch of political amateurs – too idealistic, too trusting, too "nice".' He poured scorn into the word. 'If things go on as they are they'll wake up one morning and find sans-culottes storming their parliament house and guillotines being set up in their market places. That's why they need you to open their eyes; make them see what's being planned and plotted in the Revolutionary clubs.'

The truth struck Keene like a plunge into icy water. 'You want me to be an informer, an infiltrator, an agent provocateur! Damned if I'll do that again! Stop the carriage right now!' He reached a hand to the door catch.

Challoner brought the knob of his cane down heavily on Keene's wrist. 'Stop flouncing like a prim maiden!' he snapped. 'You sold your moral virginity long ago. You're a political whore – like me! Well, no one loves a whore but she's an indispensable part of the social structure. You're good at what you do – damned good! You know the poison the Jacobins are peddling and you know their methods.'

'I also know the stratagems monarchies use to keep themselves in power.' Keene remembered bitterly the months he had spent as an informer in the radical clubs among hard-working Norfolk men who only sought some relief from the hardships of their existence; men he had betrayed and condemned to transportation or the gallows. 'I'm sick of it. That's why I want the chance to settle in a new country, a country not in the grip of cynical, self-serving politicians.'

Challoner did not respond with the sardonic laugh Keene half-expected. Instead, he shook his head with the kind of sigh that suggested a patient teacher trying to instruct a particularly dim child. 'If you really believe this Rousseauesque Utopia to be attainable, surely you will seek to do all in your power to defend it from those who want to smother it in its infancy.'

'By setting American against American?'

'No!' Challoner shouted. 'By *preventing* American being set against American. You know the sort of propaganda the French anarchists are putting out: "the Revolution ain't complete until the common people have power"; "Washington, Hamilton and the like are only a new breed of aristos, ruling in the interests of their own kind"; "any action is justified in the achievement of liberty, equality and

Derek Wilson

brotherhood". You've seen these corrosive ideas at work in France and oozing their way into England through innocent-sounding organisations – corresponding societies, constitutional clubs, friends of the people groups. Rest assured, Keene, it will happen here, without a doubt – unless you put a stop to it.'

The younger man sat back with a groan. 'In God's name, why me?'

'Because being a fugitive from British justice should give you easy entrée to radical assemblies here.'

'Fugitive! What . . . ?'

Challoner smiled and withdrew a folded sheet of parchment from his pocket. 'It was your precipitate flight that gave me the idea,' he explained, handing over the document. 'You'll see that it's a formal government note signed by Pitt, asking for help in apprehending George Keene, who is wanted in connection with seditious activities in London. Hamilton will ensure that word of this reaches the ears of Genet and his acolytes, suitably embellished with information about your pro-French sympathies, your composition and distribution of Revolutionary tracts, your infiltration of government offices, et cetera, et cetera.'

Three

K eene tried to make his abrupt departure from Germanstown as undramatic as possible, but he was aware that the suddenness of his decision appeared ungracious and came as an unfeigned disappointment to the Oaklands. He explained his leaving as a short excursion, a few months in which to explore his new homeland. In his rare optimistic moments he hoped that his absence would, indeed, be of no more than a few months' duration and that he would be able to return to the folk he had already come to regard as family. Yet it was with a feeling of black loss that he paused at a high point on the southward road to take his last look at the sprawled buildings and smoking chimneys of the homestead in which he had come to invest so much affection and aspiration. Leaving was the best thing he could do for his new friends. He could not involve them in the shame and embarrassment of harbouring an unsavoury fugitive from British justice. Perhaps, when this assignment was completed, he could return and explain, untangle misunderstandings, gradually restore trust.

Damn Challoner! Damn him to hell! Keene turned his horse's head along the muddy road that led to an uncertain future. To deprive a man once of his family was diabolical; to drive him out a second time from among his kindred was something for which the shrivelled and passionless Englishman deserved nothing less than eternal torment.

Keene did not aim to travel too far. He meant to complete his enquiries as soon as possible, and that involved getting close to Genet without undue delay. Challoner had provided him with a list of the Frenchman's known Jacobin clubs and he intended to infiltrate one of the more active, one with which the chargé d'affaires was known to be in close contact. Dover was an important farming and administrative centre eighty miles' ride south of Philadelphia on the St Jones River, which debouched into Delaware Bay. Here, according to his information, a vigorous and vociferous body had been brought into being, advocating further radical reform of the Delaware state legislature. This was where he had decided to begin his enquiries.

He rode into the town two days later on an afternoon of drowsy autumn sunshine. Dover was smaller and more compact than Philadelphia but yielded nothing to the national capital in terms of civic pride. Streets and open places had been laid out with obvious care and at the centre of the town's life there was a wide green, bordered by municipal buildings and the elegant houses of the more affluent citizens. The fact that two spacious mansions were currently under construction was testimony to the fact that some at least of those citizens continued to prosper. Everything beamed self-confident opulence.

But this was not the Dover Keene had come in search of and it did not take him long to discover the town's other face, the one she concealed behind a veil of shabby tenements. Dover was not old enough to have developed slums but it certainly had its less fashionable quarters. Here the streets were uncobbled, the houses old – some, he guessed, more than a century old; the simple residences of the earliest settlers – and, though each had once enjoyed its own spacious plot, most of the gaps between had since been filled with hastily erected cheap houses to meet the needs of immigrants and the underclass whose lot it was to minister to the needs of Dover's elite.

A few enquiries led him to a single-storey building which combined the functions of tavern, cheap lodging house and meeting place. The formidable lady who presided over the establishment known simply as Goody Mallow's, having demanded to see the contents of the stranger's purse, conveyed him to a room at the far end of a corridor. He might have it to himself for three days, his hostess explained, but if he stayed longer he would have to share it with one of her regulars, currently out of town. 'A quiet, respectable gentleman in trade,' the ample Mistress Mallow informed him, pushing a wisp of grey hair back under her bonnet.

The day was beginning to die and Keene made enquiries about supper. His hostess informed him that he might take it in the saloon at six o'clock. Having an hour to fill, he saw his horse properly stabled and then wandered the neighbourhood to get a feel of the community. The atmosphere in the darkening streets was one of leisure. Lamps hung in the shop fronts to illuminate the displays of goods, and men and women made their way unhurriedly along the sidewalks which, in the principal thoroughfares, were raised a foot above the level of the carriageway. He found a bookstall and spent several minutes surveying the volumes on offer and the people who studied them.

The proprietor clearly catered for all shades of political opinion. Alongside a stack of handsomely bound copies of Burke's *Reflections on the Revolution in France* stood a recently opened chest from which spilled several octavos of Tom Paine's riposte, *The Rights of Man*. Keene picked up one of the slim volumes and re-acquainted himself with the blistering prose of the Anglo-American protestor whose ardent quest for natural justice and a political order which could ensure it had taken him to Paris, where he had been feted by the Girondins, shared their fall and was now, according to rumour, to be seen daily in a backstreet café in sole company of a brandy bottle – bemused, maudlin and ignored.

'Very popular, that, sir.' Keene raised his eyes to discover the bookseller, a bespectacled, studious-looking man of about his own age. 'That's the two parts bound in one. Second batch I've had in. The first went quicker than hot pies. It's still got the preface.' The young man winked knowingly.

Keene smiled, encouraging the tradesman to talk. 'Preface? I'm newly arrived from England. I've only read the first part.'

'Ah, then you don't know about the storm this little volume stirred up.' The bookseller came round to Keene's side of the display table, picked up a copy of Paine's book and deftly thumbed it open at the essay following the title page. He pointed to the second paragraph and handed it to Keene. Keene read:

'The Secretary of State observes: "He is extremely pleased to find it will be reprinted here and that something is at length to be publicly said against the political heresies which have sprung up among us. He has no doubt our citizens will rally a second time round the standard of commonsense." '

Keene handed the book back. 'I'm afraid the significance eludes me . . . "political heresies" – what might they be?'

The bookseller's glasses glinted in the lamplight as he eagerly launched into an explanation. 'Well, you see, sir, the publisher of the American edition – dedicated to President Washington – included this endorsement by Mr Jefferson, the Secretary of State; only Mr Jefferson protested that he never intended his imprimatur to be publicised in this way. Well, the President was furious. According to the press, the old friendship between him and the Secretary of State has broken down completely.'

'And these "heresies"?'

'Well, now,' the young man lowered his voice and leaned forward, 'no mystery there. By heresies Mr Jefferson means the opinions of Mr Hamilton and his party.'

Two other browsers had been listening to this conversation and one of them, a middle-aged man in a grubby wig and a stained, faded greatcoat, now joined in. 'Have a care, John. Our visitor here is from the "mother country".' He spoke the words with a sneer. 'Perhaps he shares friend Hamilton's passion for monarchy.'

Keene turned to face the speaker and saw a fleshy, high-coloured, choleric face with heavy brows over dark, humourless eyes. His whole appearance suggested that he was not a man to tangle with. Normally Keene would have brushed aside the snub but he realised that an opportunity had presented itself sooner than he had expected to draw attention to himself. He decided on truculence.

'It's you, sir, who should have a care not to display your ignorance, nor to be so free with your insults. All Englishman are not tarred with the same brush. We don't need to ask leave of Americans to think for ourselves.' He paused long enough to see the older man narrow his eyes in anger before turning his back and taking up another book.

The stranger muttered something about 'arrogant Englishmen' but allowed himself to be drawn away from the shop by his companion.

The proprietor, who had diplomatically retreated into the inner recesses of his shop, now re-emerged and approached Keene with mingled deference and anxiety. 'May I ask, sir, whether you intend to stay long in Dover?'

Keene decided to maintain the pose of affronted guest. 'That depends how many of Dover's citizens are as churlish as the gentleman who has just left.'

The young man drew him somewhat theatrically on one side and spoke quietly, although there was now no one within earshot. 'If you plan to spend much time among us, sir, you'd be wise to have a care of Gabriel Jensen.'

'And to whom, sir, am I indebted for this warning?' Keene deliberately raised his voice, as if to make quite clear that he cared not who heard him.

The other man offered a timid bow. 'John Bowman, at your service, sir.'

'I'm George Keene. And why must I go in fear and trembling of this boor who calls himself Gabriel Jensen? Is he one of your town elders?'

Bowman allowed his serious features to be surprised by a slight smile. 'Jensen? Goodness no. Though doubtless he'd like to have public office.' He paused, debating within himself, Keene imagined, just how indiscreet he might allow himself to be. 'You should understand that there are political . . .' he struggled to find the appropriate word . . . 'cross-currents here. This nation believes in free speech . . . '

Keene nodded. 'That's one reason why I have come. If democracy can flourish anywhere it will be in this country.'

'It's a virtue that brings many here. But when every man speaks his mind what man can make himself heard? On every conceivable issue there are a dozen arguments clamouring to gain attention – national government versus federal government; two-chamber assembly versus one chamber; slavery versus anti-slavery; pro-French versus pro-British. Usually it's the loudest mouths rather than the coolest heads that attract the biggest following.'

'And Jensen has a particularly loud mouth?'

Bowman nodded solemnly. 'Aye, that he has – and other ways of persuading men to his point of view. If I were you I'd keep out of his path until you've got a clearer understanding of how things work here.'

'Well, I thank you for your advice, Mr Bowman. And I'll take a copy of Tom Paine's book.' Keene handed over the necessary coins. 'Whether I'll heed your warning I doubt. I've braved King George and his so-called justice and it's having an untamed tongue that's brought me across the ocean. I ain't about to put a curb on it for fear of offending some provincial tub-thumper.'

The bookseller winced and shrugged. 'Well, Mr Keene, I wish you a peaceful stay in Dover – and don't forget to call here whenever you're looking for the current books and pamphlets. Fresh consignments of the current publications almost every week.'

Keene walked thoughtfully back to Goody Mallow's. He entered the saloon, a long room with a bar at one end, around which several men were clustered drinking, and a dozen tables set for dining or card play occupying the rest of the space. He sat at a table in the far corner from where he could observe and be observed and, while he waited for his food, he opened *The Rights of Man*, giving every appearance of studying it intently with the aid of a lamp hanging from the ceiling above. It took no time at all for him to become the object of common curiosity. From the occasional nods and glances in his direction it became obvious that the stranger in town was attracting much speculation.

It was when he had disposed of a bowl of mutton stew and was mopping up the last pools of gravy with a hunk of rye bread that a tall man in a dark blue coat over white breeches and well-polished boots detached himself from his companions and strolled casually to his table carrying a bottle and a couple of tumblers.

'Will you permit me, sir, to drink the health of a newcomer to our fair city?' The man had an engaging smile but Keene was very conscious of being scrutinised carefully by his pale blue eyes.

'A traveller always welcomes a civil greeting.' The Englishman motioned the newcomer to a chair.

Coiling himself on to the slightly rickety piece of furniture, the tall man introduced himself. 'Jake Featherby. I work in the Justice Department.' He poured two generous measures of a bronze liquid.

'George Keene, newly arrived from England,' Keene responded. He took a mouthful of the rough spirit. 'Justice Department.' His voice took on a cynical timbre. 'I assume that involves policing the inhabitants of your fair city and keeping an eye on new arrivals.'

Featherby's thin face remained impassive. 'I assume, Mr Keene, that you have no need for anxiety on that score.' His eyes flickered momentarily towards the book which still lay open beside Keene's plate. 'Are you staying with us or passing through?'

'I guess that depends on what Dover has to offer. My funds won't last for ever. I must find honest employment soon.'

'Dover always has need of educated men and I take you for something of a scholar.'

Keene shrugged. 'My studies have all been in the university of life.'

'You've travelled much?'

'Italy, Austria, Prussia, the Netherlands, France.'

'I envy you, Mr Keene. You speak all those languages?'

Keene laughed. 'Only French well. The others enough to make myself understood.'

Featherby refilled the glasses. 'You must be familiar with what is happening in France. We get bits of news here from time to time but they're pretty confused. My impression is that their Revolution has turned sour on them. Are things really as chaotic as we hear?'

Keene sipped his drink and felt the harsh, locally distilled liquor sear his throat. When he replied it was with theatrical caution. 'Everyone I meet over here wants to know what's happening in Europe. I must confess that surprises me. I thought you people had turned your back on the Old World.'

The tall man leaned forward, arms folded on the table. 'I'll let you into a secret, Mr Keene.' He adopted a mock-conspiratorial tone. 'There isn't a man in Delaware who isn't a politician. You see my friends at the bar?' He nodded towards the group at the other end of the room and as Keene looked in that direction he saw, from the corner of his eye, his companion top up his glass. 'Every one of them could explain to you the constitution of the state and the nation – and tell you exactly what was wrong with both.' He stood up suddenly. 'But don't take my word for it; come and meet them.'

As Featherby turned, Keene deftly emptied the contents of his tumbler into the jug of ale he had ordered to accompany his meal. Following his companion across the room, he could already feel the alcohol relaxing his leg muscles. Well, he thought, if that was Featherby's game he would play along. Halfway across the room he stumbled against a chair and grabbed a table for support, sending a fellow guest's tankard crashing to the floor. The man jumped up with an oath and Keene slurred his apology. Featherby soothed the customer and insisted on paying for a new drink.

At the bar Keene was surrounded by half a dozen Delawarians eager to introduce themselves and shake his hand. Once more he found his fingers encircling a glass of the aggressive local spirit and, with several pairs of eyes upon him, it was all he could do to make sure that most of the liquid ended up on the sawdust at his feet. Featherby and his friends plied him with questions and drink in equally generous measure. Was this, Keene wondered, their normal treatment of strangers, or did the interrogation suggest that they knew or suspected that he was not what he seemed? Whatever the truth, all he could do was try to keep a clear head, play the innocent and pick up any snippets of information they might let fall.

He allowed his answers to their questions to flow more freely and indiscreetly as the evening wore on. Did he think the restoration of law and order in France was irretrievable? They should not believe all the wild stories spread by the enemies of the republic. Would Pitt send British troops to fight the Revolutionaries? He was sure the British people would never go to war to restore a corrupt monarchical regime. Was it not true, then, as they had heard, that France was in the grip of an anarchy far worse than anything that had preceded it? Only, he insisted, with growing belligerence, if rule by the people was dubbed 'anarchy'. Certainly there had been a great deal of blood-letting but what could one expect when the mass of Frenchmen had been subjected to generations of organised violence by the privileged minority? What of the prospect of Revolutionary ideas spreading to other countries?

As Keene leaned back against the bar for support and gave every appearance of focusing with difficulty on his interrogators he was very aware that they were all waiting with acute interest for his answer. He decided to give them good value. 'Never forget what Rousseau said.' He waggled a finger at them in a very fluid gesture. '"The fruits of the earth belong to us all and the earth itself belongs to no one." What you call the spread of Revolution is inev . . . inev . . . can't be stopped. France and America are its co-founders but it has no national boundaries.' From beneath half-closed lids Keene watched the townsmen exchange knowing glances.

He judged that this would be a good moment to make his exit. He yawned, released his grip on the counter and stood, swaying slightly. 'Gentlemen, I must bid you adieu.' He took a pace forward. His knees buckled and he would have fallen to the floor if strong arms had not caught him.

'We must get him to his bed.'

'Better to let the anarchist pig spend the night in jail.'

'No need for that. It'll only attract attention.'

'Yes, we want him moved out of town before Belmont and his mob find out about him.'

Keene listened to the discussion which accompanied his progress, half walking, half dragged, along the corridor to his room. There he was dumped unceremoniously on the bed.

As soon as he heard the shuffling footsteps retreat again down the corridor he sat up, though not without an effort. The crude aqua vitae, for all his efforts to restrict his intake, still muddied his brain. Try as he might to assemble his thoughts into a coherent pattern and analyse what he had learned since his arrival in Dover, the several elements refused to do any more than blunder around inside his tired skull. He fell back upon the pillow. Tomorrow all would be clear.

So it proved, though not in the way that Keene had expected.

Four

H e was shaken into consciousness by a rough and insist-
ent hand on his shoulder and found himself blearily
looking up into the flabby features of Goody Mallow. Both
her words and actions proclaimed indignation bordering
on anger.

'Up you get!' (shake). 'Up and out!' (violent shake). 'I'll
not have you here an instant longer!' (pummel). 'Out of my
house as soon as you're dressed!' (tweaking the bedclothes).

Exposed to the gaze of an irate matron and clad only in his
shirt, Keene felt at a distinct disadvantage. He grabbed the
counterpane around him and sat up with a pathetic attempt to
salvage some dignity. 'What's the meaning of this, madam?'

'Don't madam me!' The hostess stood back a pace,
sneering down at him over the bulwark of her massive
bosom. 'I've had dealings with your smooth-talking sort
before. I'll not have troublemaking foreigners under my
roof. Out within ten minutes or I have you thrown out!'
With that Mistress Mallow stalked from the room, leaving
the door open behind her.

Keene rose and grimaced at himself in the washstand
mirror, noting as he did so that no water had been set out for
him. He briefly contemplated calling back the proprietress
to demand this courtesy but decided not to provoke another
tirade. No matter; his unshaven appearance would add to the
pariah image he was here to project.

He brushed his long fair hair, dressed, carefully tied his
cravat. Again, he surveyed his image in the mirror. The coat,
good quality but creased; the shirt, in need of laundering; the

chin, stubbled. What did they amount to? An Englishman of some standing now running to seed. Perhaps there was more than a surface resemblance between the reflection and the reality. Was there anything left of George Keene? Or had he become the counterfeit his masters wanted him to present to the world? Where was the boy whose little world had been bounded by the fields, meadows and woods of his Norfolk home and expected to spend all his days on the land in semi-poverty? That child had existed half a dozen lifetimes ago. Between him and the scruffy man in the mirror lay a succession of metamorphoses. Like some doomed butterfly, he was compelled to return time and again to the chrysalis, always emerging with a different shape and colour. Was there no breaking out of the cycle? He had tried. He had served Challoner's interests faithfully in the hope that the little grey man would honour his promise to release him once his mission was accomplished. All he had gained from that was the realisation that Challoner had a somewhat restricted understanding of the word 'honour'. He had escaped to America only to discover that there was no escape. Keene scowled at the insubstantial image before him. No escape and no identity, save the transitory role his paymaster assigned him.

'Mr Keene!' The name bellowed down the corridor in a reverberating contralto shook him from his reverie. He stuffed his few possessions into his saddlebag and strode from the room. At the front door of her establishment Mistress Mallow barred his way, hand outstretched. Keene thrust a coin into the palm and smiled as the recipient examined it with patent suspicion. 'I thank you, ma'am, for your gracious hospitality,' he announced with a mocking bow and enjoyed the woman's half gasp half grunt as he stepped into the street.

Keene found a smart coffee house close to the centre of the town where he could order some breakfast. The room was lightly populated at this early hour. Two negro waiters with white aprons over their grubby clothes moved with a casual grace serving food and drink to the dozen or so patrons and wiping down the tables in a desultory fashion. Keene helped himself to a copy of the *Dover Gazette* from the rack by the door and ordered coffee, bread and cheese. He scanned the broadsheet for any items that might fill in more details of the local political situation. There was no doubting the newspaper's editorial stance, which, if last night's experience was anything to go by, represented the attitude of Dover's leading citizens.

> The outrageous activities of Mr Genet, the French chargé d'affaires, continue unabated. We understand that, despite official protests of the strongest nature delivered in the name of President Washington, the representative of the government in Paris continues to provoke discord between this nation and our neighbours.
>
> According to sources close to the State Department, Mr Genet's agents are recruiting and arming a battalion in Kentucky to aid the French-speaking inhabitants of Louisiana in an insurrection against their Spanish rulers. The *Gazette* has never supported the maintenance of colonial control in any part of this continent but neither will we countenance interference in the affairs of our neighbours. Such interference can only provoke repercussions of a diplomatic – and, perhaps, military – nature.
>
> As we have pointed out repeatedly, Mr Genet's provocative actions are designed to stir up disaffected elements within the states of the Union and to overthrow the constitution we have laboured hard and long to achieve. His countrymen have, lamentably, had anarchy forced upon them. Americans have no wish to be hustled down the same road. We call upon our leaders, both here and in Philadelphia, especially those who, like Mr Jefferson and Mr Monroe, have been loudest in their admiration of

the French Revolution, to reaffirm this nation's neutrality in the European conflict and to reject unequivocally the attempts to embroil us in it. They could start by demanding Mr Genet's recall.

Keene turned to the inside pages of the *Gazette* to see if there was any news from England. His eye fell on the following brief communiqué:

Yesterday, 13 November, the French merchant ship *Marie Chantelle*, Captain Williams, having been despatched to the island of San Domingue in the grip of insurrection, arrived in Charleston with a further batch of refugees. The 175 men, women and children aboard bring to more than two thousand the total number of planters and their families forced to flee from their homes since the abolition of slavery in the French colony. The latest arrivals bring more reports of atrocities perpetrated by the black hordes who appear to have taken complete control of the country. We shall have more information in our next edition.

A sudden crash interrupted Keene's reading. He lowered the paper to discover the cause. By the street door one of the waiters was staring horrified at a scattering of broken pottery at his feet. It was immediately obvious what had happened. A new customer, blundering carelessly into the coffee house, had swung the door into the waiter causing him to drop his loaded tray.

'Out of my path, you clumsy nigger!' the newcomer shouted, crunching his way across the debris.

The commotion brought the proprietress bustling from the back premises, carrying a soup ladle. She took in the situation at a glance, strode up to the negro and swung her implement at his head with all the force she could muster. The man cowered and held up his arm but was too slow to fend off the blow. The ladle drew blood from a gash on his cheek but that did not assuage the woman's fury. 'Damned nigger!' she screamed, beating him again and again. 'Do you think I've money to waste on the best English crockery just to have it smashed by useless slaves? It's back in chains for you and no food for three days. Get in there!' She pushed him towards the inner door. 'I'll teach you, you damned bungling . . .' The rest of her diatribe was cut off by the closing of the door behind her.

In the hush following the storm Keene poured himself more coffee from a creamware jug made in the English potteries and decorated with the American flag – a circle of stars and horizontal bands of red and white. He stared into the black liquid. 'Slavery'. 'Freedom'. What did the words mean? Liberty made a compelling slogan but was it any more than that? Not in France; that much was clear. For a shivering moment he relived the horrors of La Conciergerie, that overcrowded prison crammed with all sorts of men, women and children, united only in their common destination – the guillotine. Prisoners marked out for fake trials and predetermined condemnation by a regime whose manifesto had been set out in the Declaration of the Rights of Man and of the Citizen. 'All men are born free and equal' that document had bravely asserted, specifying the inviolability of the individual from coercion and arbitrary arrest.

Not in Britain either, where a panic-stricken ruling class sent soldiers to break up meetings of peaceful artisans, and members of parliament laughed at one of their number, William Wilberforce, when he attempted to introduce a bill outlawing the slave trade. Nor even, it seemed, in this land to which, for two hundred years, men had fled in pursuit of the will-o'-the-wisp freedom and spilled a generation's blood to break with the tyranny of London. Now here they were, standing in righteous condemnation of the black inhabitants of San Domingue for casting aside their own slavery. It was two years since the plantation workers of France's sugar-rich colony had begun their revolt. And who had tried to quell it and rushed to the aid of the white landowners? The French. And the British. And the Americans. 'Liberty'? 'Thraldom'? Two sides of a coin. You tossed it and hoped that it would fall favourably for you.

Keene turned his attention to his own problem. He had made himself persona non grata with some of the more respectable members of Dover society, and doubtless Featherby and his cronies would already be spreading the word that George Keene was a man to be watched. If Hamilton had done his job properly it would already be known in official circles that the loud-mouthed Englishman was a fugitive from British justice. His notoriety was, therefore, spreading satisfactorily, and must, sooner or later, draw him to the attention of the republican activists he had come here to locate. But that could take time and he was determined to complete his assignment as soon as possible. To complete it, deliver his report, and then disappear – permanently this time. North America was a large continent and the frontiers of settlement were constantly being pushed further westwards as people went in search of land and liberty. He would complete the work he had agreed to do, then put himself beyond the reach of Challoner's waving tentacles.

He pushed aside his empty plate. Time to take positive action. He had two names to follow up: Jensen and Belmont. There was one place where he could begin his enquiries.

A brisk ten-minute walk brought him to John Bowman's bookshop. At this early hour there were no other shoppers or browsers on the premises and Keene found the young proprietor presiding solemnly over the shelves of gathered wit and wisdom from behind a tall desk. He slipped down from his high stool and gazed at his customer over the rim of his glasses. 'Mr Keene, back so soon?' The welcome did not seem to be altogether enthusiastic.

Keene offered a frank, disarming smile. 'A stranger in town needs friendly guidance and you were kind enough to make free with your advice yesterday.'

The young man walked over to the shop door, looked briefly outside, then closed it before turning to face Keene. 'If I may say so, Mr Keene, you seem better at listening to advice than following it.'

'Meaning?'

'Your lack of caution when discussing politics seems to have earned you some important enemies within hours of your arrival.'

'News travels fast in Dover.'

'"Ill news hath wings and with the wind doth go" – Michael Drayton; some think him as fine a poet as Shakespeare. What's your opinion, Mr Keene?'

'I must bow to your greater knowledge, Mr Bowman. But as to last night's events . . . '

The bookseller was not listening. He seemed agitated by Keene's presence, yet unwilling to deprive himself of it. He took his visitor by the arm and led him deeper into the shop. 'You perhaps don't realise how very intriguing a new arrival from England is for us. We see so few. After the war, of course, your countrymen were not at all welcome. Now?' He shrugged. 'Memories fade. Our leaders preach the normalisation of relationships. But there are still those whose scars run deep.'

Keene nodded. 'Wars don't end when the last shot has been fired or the last signature added to the treaty. Too many people have lost fathers or sons . . . '

'Exactly.' Bowman nodded solemnly. 'So, many of us are cautious about the English; some still hostile; all curious.'

'And you?' Keene asked, warming to this studious young philosopher. 'What do you think of King George's merry men?'

Bowman sighed and leaned against a bookstack. 'My two older brothers were killed at the Battle of Monmouth Courthouse. I was only ten at the time and they were no more than boys. 28 June '78. That day destroyed our family. My mother was determined to keep me away from the fighting. My father insisted it was my duty to train as a soldier so that I could avenge the deaths of his other sons. When the war ended before I could enlist he somehow felt cheated. He began drinking heavily and that clouded his thinking. He became convinced that Bobby and Mike were heroes and I was a coward. I guess it didn't help that I developed into the scholar of the family, more interested in books than hunting and trapping and long treks into the wilderness. Eventually he threw me out.'

Keene said quietly, 'Then you must be among those whose scars run deep.'

The bookseller shook his head. '"Canst thou not minister to a mind diseased." You're familiar with *Macbeth*:

> "Pluck from the memory a rooted sorrow,
> Raze out the written troubles of the brain?"

'You know the answer to the question:

> "Therein the patient must minister to himself."

'I left New Jersey. Eventually found my way here. Built up this little business. Healed myself with work and the company of all my friends.' He waved a hand at the crowded bookshelves. 'God willing, I have more years ahead than lie behind. If the past is a poisoned cup, why continue drinking from it?'

Keene felt so much at one with this sage young man that he found it difficult to keep up his masquerade. After a long silence, he said briskly, 'It's unfortunate that we can't all retire from the stirring events of the time. Some of us, to use your metaphor, must tread the grapes for tomorrow's wine.' In his mind Keene could hear Challoner speaking those words and he hated himself for mouthing them. 'I was hoping, Mr Bowman, that you could give me a little information. Where might I find a Mr Belmont?'

The bookseller sighed. 'That's information you can easily come by. There's no reason why I shouldn't tell you. Auguste

Belmont is the French consul here. I'll give you his address.'
He walked back to his desk, took up a pen and scribbled a
few words on a scrap of paper.

Keene remained at the back of the shop, casting an
appraising eye over the spines of the books displayed.
'That fellow Jensen,' he called out. 'What can you tell
me about him?'

Suddenly he heard the handle of the shop door being
rattled. At the same moment Bowman whispered urgently,
'Stay where you are! Keep out of sight.'

From the deep shadow in a corner formed by two bookshelves he heard the proprietor unlock the door and welcome
a customer.

'Good morning to you, Mr Featherby.'

'Morning, John. You're late opening up today.'

'Truth to tell, I was catching up on a bit of stocktaking
and quite forgot the time. What may I find for you?'

Keene heard the older man's footsteps and when Featherby
replied he did so from just the other side of the stack behind
which Keene was hiding.

'Not what, John; who. Do you recognise this little book?'

'Yes,' Bowman spoke cautiously. '*The Rights of Man*,
latest edition.'

'Pernicious stuff, but I'll allow you're quite within your
rights to stock it. In fact this copy is from your stock. You
sold it yesterday to a visitor; an Englishman.'

'That's right, I remember.'

'Good. Do you recall anything else about him?'

'Such as what, Mr Featherby?'

'Such as his name and what his business might be in
Dover.'

There was a long pause before Bowman responded, as
though deep in thought. 'Name? Yes, he did tell me. What
was it? King, I think.'

'Are you sure it wasn't Keene?'

'That's right, Keene. I'm afraid I didn't take much notice.
There were several customers in the shop at the time.'

'So you didn't engage him in your usual friendly conversation?'

'As I said, I was busy. What's so important about this fellow?'

'It seems that our Mr Keene is something of a notorious celebrity, an anarchist troublemaker. He's wanted for sedition in his own country. The last thing we need is him stirring up unrest here.'

'What are you going to do with him?'

'Put him on the next ship back to England.' Featherby laughed. 'Unless some of our more zealous citizens decide to save King George's hangman a job. But we have to catch him first. Last night we knew where he was and we'd discovered something about his Revolutionary ideas and pro-French sympathies. I simply intended to have him closely watched, as a matter of routine. It wasn't till this morning that the Governor called me in and passed on the latest news from Philadelphia. It seems the President has a personal interest in apprehending this Keene and sending him back to face British justice. A useful diplomatic gesture, I suppose. Unfortunately, by the time I got to Keene's lodging house he had already been thrown out by an indignant landlady. So momentarily we've lost track of him.'

Keene listened anxiously. How would Bowman respond to this official approach? If he believed Featherby he would surely have no reason to risk the anger of the authorities by harbouring a wanted criminal. And if he did his duty as a good citizen Keene might well find himself in chains and at sea before he could get word to Hamilton.

Bowman was speaking again. 'So why are you seeking your quarry here?'

Featherby ignored the question. 'You won't mind if I just have a quick look around?'

'My door's been locked. How . . . '

'I wasn't suggesting that you'd be so foolish as to harbour him, John. But he might be skulking out back of your shop.'

46

Keene looked around desperately for a means of concealment or escape. Immediately behind him there was an internal door. Could he get through it quickly and silently? He put his hand to the knob. It was stiff. Moreover the wood fitted tight against the frame. He was about to throw secrecy to the winds and yank the door open when he heard Bowman call out.

'He's there!'

'Where!' the voice of Featherby demanded.

'Across the street! I'm sure I saw him go down that alleyway!'

There were sounds of rapid movement from the front of the shop and Keene heard the door pulled open hurriedly. Immediately, Bowman appeared round the edge of the bookstack.

'You heard all that,' he whispered. 'Quick, through that door and across the kitchen! There's a way out to the back lane. Hurry! You've only got seconds.'

'Thank you,' Keene muttered but was cut short by the bookseller.

'No time for that. GO!'

Keene stumbled through the doorway. He rushed across the room beyond to the exit in the far wall. He stepped out into a narrow, rutted lane and looked quickly both ways. To the right the passageway ended after fifty yards in an expanse of open grass. He ran in that direction.

He had only gone a few paces when two men appeared round the corner ahead. Keene abruptly slowed to a casual walk. He drew level with the strangers and, with a smile and a nod, stood aside to let them pass. In the next instant they stepped up to him and each grabbed an arm in a rigid grip. Keene struggled but was no match for his silent adversaries. They forced him back the way he had come. Within seconds he was once more in the bookshop.

John Bowman stood by his desk, eyes downcast. Beside him, leaning against a bookstack, Featherby smiled triumphantly. 'John, John, John, I am disappointed in you. Disappointed but not surprised.'

Five

Keene tried bluster. 'What do you mean by treating visitors like this! I haven't broken any of your laws!'

'Save it for the courthouse,' Featherby languidly replied. 'You can have your say there. We believe in free speech in this country.'

The words rang hollow in Keene's brain ten minutes later, when he and Bowman, their hands bound behind them, were hustled into an open cart for their short journey to jail. As he stared out at the passing townsfolk, several of whom stopped to jeer and wave their fists, he thought of those other wagons, the Paris tumbrils, trundling through hysterical crowds to the Conciergerie or the Place du Carousel with their doomed human cargoes. All regimes exercised control in the name of the people or, more grandly, of freedom or justice. And all had one concern above all others – the preservation of the ruling elite.

The little procession made its way along the road flanking the wide grassed area in front of the impressive new state house, topped by its elegant white bell-tower. It circuited the adjacent government buildings and came to halt beside a narrow rear entrance. A row of barred ground-floor windows left Keene in no doubt about the purpose of this part of the complex.

Five minutes later he and his fellow prisoner were on the other side of one of those windows and watching the heavy iron-studded door of their cell slam shut. Bowman slumped down on one of the two rickety beds. Keene sat opposite him, the knees of the two men almost touching in the confined space.

'I'm sorry to have got you into this,' Keene said.

Bowman shrugged. 'I got myself into it. I could have just handed you over.'

'Why didn't you?'

The bookseller's face wrinkled in a puzzled frown. 'I've been asking myself the same question. I guess it's because I loathe Featherby and all he stands for.'

'Tell me about him,' Keene suggested.

The other man paused, collecting his thoughts. 'Jacob Featherby,' he said eventually, in carefully measured tones, 'is a born politician. Of humanity, compassion, the aspirations of man's spirit he knows nothing. His study has been entirely in "the bloody book of law". He's ambitious. His sights are firmly set on high national office and there's little doubt that he'll get there.'

'What's his job here, exactly?'

'Officially, he's just one of the lawyers in the Justice Department. Unofficially, he's the governor's bloodhound. He licks his master's hand and sniffs out his master's suspected enemies and rivals.'

'Which category do I come in?'

Bowman removed his spectacles and rubbed the lenses on the sleeve of his jacket. 'There's something else you should know about Featherby: he's a fanatic.'

'I've already had evidence of . . .'

The scholarly American was too intent on his own line of thought to listen. 'This Robespierre who's cock of the walk in France and washing the streets in blood – I hear he's a lawyer.'

'Yes.' Vivid images flashed into Keene's mind: ragged sans-culotte mobs chanting '*Vive Robespierre!*' as they marched excitedly to the place of execution; the great citizen's elegant coach attended by mounted National Guards as it was cheered through the streets of Paris; the look of fear his name brought to the eyes of men and women who had

Derek Wilson

fallen foul of the Committee of Public Safety. He had never come face to face with the embodiment of the Terror but the spirit of Robespierre permeated the city so that Keene felt he knew the man intimately.

'Odd, isn't it,' Bowman observed reflectively, readjusting his glasses, 'that men brought up to revere the law can believe that the law can be defended by means that are quite outside the law.'

The same thought had often struck Keene and he had to steel himself not to show warm agreement with his companion. 'Robespierre is a man driven by the principles of natural justice. I doubt the same may be said of Featherby.'

Bowman shook his head firmly. 'Oh, you're wrong there. "Brutus is an honourable man". Everything he does is for the good of the people, the security of the state.' For the first time his words became hard-edged with cynical humour.

'Including throwing innocent booksellers into jail?'

The American laughed. 'Oh, he's convinced that I'm a disruptive influence. He's been looking for an opportunity to close down the shop for a couple of years now. This is a real triumph for him.'

'And are you . . . a disruptive influence?'

'Only if upholding the rights of free speech and free publication enshrined in our constitution is a threat to public order.'

'I'm sorry I provided Featherby with the chance he was looking for.'

Bowman shrugged. 'He'd have made some excuse, sooner or later. Failing that his little private militia would have found some means of putting me out of business. A mysterious fire, perhaps, or an attack by "highwaymen" on some lonely stretch of road.' He looked up, fixing shrewd eyes on Keene. 'But what of you? Are you . . . a disruptive influence?'

The Englishman had well rehearsed the details of his 'identity'. 'Only if meeting with the poor and oppressed to help them find ways to improve themselves is a threat to public order. I belonged to a couple of London societies – the Corresponding Society, the Society of the Friends of the People – peaceful organisations, pledged to the open dissemination of ideas and working for change through parliamentary activity. After what had happened here in America and what was still happening in France it was only natural that intelligent men wanted to ask questions about how and why they were governed. But, of course, to those in power this was "revolution"; this was "French anarchy"; this was plunging down the steep slope to chaos. Dear God! What is revolutionary about ideas proposed by John Locke a hundred years ago?'

'"Men are by nature free, equal and independent and no man can be subjected to the power of another without his own consent",' Bowman quoted.

'Exactly. And, "Absolute monarchy is inconsistent with civil society".'

'And, "There remains in the people a supreme power to remove or alter the government when they find the government act contrary to the trust reposed in them".'

'Just so. These were the principles which underlay the bid for American independence.'

'For which your king and some of your parliamentarians have never forgiven us.'

'It certainly upset them – but not as much as the guillotining of Louis XVI. Now the political establishment is convinced that free speech must lead inevitably to royal and aristocratic blood flowing in the gutters. So they try to stop it by infiltrating the clubs, using agents provocateurs and agitators, sending troops to break up meetings, seizing "inflammatory" pamphlets, putting their authors on trial for sedition, sending simple men off to the penal colonies. What they can't understand is that it is these actions which will provoke the very revolution they so much dread.'

Bowman brought his hands together in silent applause, 'A fine speech, Mr Keene, and one which, I imagine, you've delivered often. Was it for that that you were driven to seek refuge here?'

Keene smiled. 'Worse than that; I published a weekly paper, *The Talisman*. It propagated some of the lectures delivered to radical societies in London and Manchester. It urged people to organise petitions demanding annual parliaments, universal suffrage, abolition of rotten and pocket boroughs. That didn't please our lords and masters. They sent thugs to smash the press. We found another printer and continued operating from secret premises. It was when they realised that they couldn't silence *The Talisman* that they issued a writ for my arrest. Fortunately I'm not without friends in high places. They tipped me the wink. So, here I am.'

Keene felt rather proud of his story. It had the ring of truth because all its individual components were true. The radical clubs *did* exist; so did *The Talisman*; violent reactionary opposition – both open and covert – *was* becoming fiercer month by month. Challoner's paymasters *were* in a state of near panic at the growth of open dissent and the connections between British malcontents and their French counterparts.

Bowman lay back on the thin, grimy mattress. 'A stirring tale, Mr Keene. I'm sorry your bid for freedom has come to such an abrupt end. But tell me, were you merely seeking asylum here or planning to continue your crusade?'

'As to that, Mr Bowman, I trust you'll forgive me if I keep my own counsel. It's for your safety. If Featherby and his crew interrogate you it will be better that you can honestly say you have little acquaintance with me and know nothing of my plans.'

After that, conversation became desultory. Each man locked himself into his own thoughts. Keene was preoccupied in trying to find a way out of his predicament. If he were returned to London the chances of ever being able to escape from Challoner's clutches were virtually zero. Perhaps he could throw himself on the mercy of the Dover court; point out that, like the new nation itself, he was only casting off the shackles of repressive, undemocratic government. If he could convince them that he was no threat to the stability of the State of Delaware they might restore his liberty. But he had to acknowledge, ruefully, that he had been hoist on his own petard. The act he had been putting on since his arrival in Dover – of a committed revolutionary on the run – had been manifestly effective.

The day passed and the following night. The prisoners talked sometimes, slept sometimes, ate when sparse but surprisingly palatable victuals were brought to them. They saw no one except their jailer, and he was uncommunicative. When questioned about how long they were to be detained or when they would be taken before the judge he responded with a shrug of his massive shoulders and a facial expression that indicated that he was totally indifferent to the fate of his charges. In fact, they did not have to wait long. On the afternoon following their arrest they were taken via a series of internal passages to the courtroom.

The first thing that impressed Keene was the crowd. The large chamber ran the full width of the building and the back half of it was given over to public benches. These were crammed with a motley assemblage of men and women, whose attentive demeanour suggested that they were more than mere members of an audience, come to watch the workings of justice: they were participants in a corporate civic drama. They were like – and yet not like – their counterparts in Paris. It was a mere four months since he had stood before the Revolutionary tribunal, being screamed at by a sweating mob who had come there for no other purpose than to hound to death the presumed enemies of the people. These Delaware citizens were quiet in their demeanour. They sat, for the most part sombrely dressed, attentive to the proceedings and discussing them among themselves in undertones. But in common with France's children of the Revolution they were not a bit overawed by the legal process. Keene sensed that they 'owned' what went on in this place. In England the robed and wigged dispensers of royal justice were there to impress miscreants and spectators alike with their high-flown language and arcane rituals. Here the citizenry had come to share in, to endorse, almost to hold to account those who exercised judicial power in the name of the people.

The judge, who presided from behind a desk set upon a rostrum only slightly raised above the common floor level, was a tall, sad-eyed man in his fifties. He was disposing in short order of a case of common assault when Keene and Bowman were ushered into the courtroom. After the convicted man was returned to the cells there was a short intermission during which the two new defendants were conveyed to a stand in front of one of the tall windows flanking the hall. Scores of eyes scrutinised them, some, Keene thought, with sympathy, while others conveyed hostility, suspicion or frank curiosity.

There was no doubting the demeanour of Jake Featherby, who bustled into the room through a side door and glowered briefly at the prisoners as he waved a junior colleague to vacate the central position at a long desk on the opposite side of the room and, after shuffling a pile of papers self-importantly, rose to address the court.

'Your honour, I have the privilege of presenting the state's indictment in the next two cases, which are linked.'

The judge referred to his papers. 'Mr Bowman and Mr Keene?'

'Yes, your honour.'

'They are not charged with the same offence, are they?'

'No, your honour, but—'

'Then I will consider them separately.'

Featherby's expressionless face concealed his reaction but there was a hint of irritation in his voice. 'I will show that the man Keene is a seditionist and that he was harboured by Bowman.'

Now it was the judge's turn to register annoyance. 'You will be asking me for an order to detain Mr Keene for trial on a charge of sedition but you do not intend to prefer the same charge against Mr Bowman?'

'That is correct, your honour.'

'If Mr Keene's guilt has not been established how can Mr Bowman be indicted as an accessory?'

'He attempted to prevent Keene's arrest.'

'Had a warrant been obtained for Mr Keene's arrest?'

'No, your honour, but—'

'Then Mr Bowman was not in defiance of the law.'

'Your honour, I must protest . . .' The tall lawyer was now red-faced with scarcely suppressed anger.

The judge raised his voice just sufficiently to block Featherby's response. 'Mr Featherby, I will not have my time wasted nor our citizens harassed by over-zealous, self-appointed guardians of the public weal. We do not have an Inquisition in this state and, please God, we never shall.'

The lawyer opened his mouth to reply but the judge ignored him and turned to the prisoners. 'Mr Bowman, you have no charge to face at this time and may leave the court. However, if Mr Keene is subsequently found guilty of an offence against the laws of the State of Delaware, you may be called upon to face charges in connection with the said offence. Meanwhile, I counsel you to be careful in your choice of friends. Now, Mr Featherby, what have you to tell me about Mr Keene?'

There was a murmur of excited chatter along the public benches as the bookseller made his way from the courtroom. Featherby used the hiatus to regain his composure. He sat down and sifted his papers, avoiding eye contact with the presiding officer. Only when the judge said, with a fixed smile, 'I await your pleasure, sir,' did he rise to his feet and, hand on lapel, speak with a loud, sharp-edged voice.

'Your honour, Delaware is known as the first state of the Union. It is something of which all its people are rightly proud. Caesar Rodney's ride to Philadelphia in 1776 broke the tie in the Convention and secured the vote for independence. In 1787 this state was the first to ratify the constitution . . . '

The judge leaned forward. 'There is, I assume, some point to this history lesson.'

'Yes indeed, your honour. I simply make the point that the laws of the Union and of the State of Delaware are inextricably intertwined. The freedoms of our people and of those who live in the other twelve states stand or fall together and it is our solemn duty to defend both our laws and our freedoms. This demands constant vigilance and at no time is that vigilance more necessary than the present.'

Keene watched the man warming to his theme and remembered Bowman's description: 'fanatic'.

'Your honour knows as well as I the appalling events which are now tearing apart the French nation. But perhaps your honour is less aware that what is happening in the land of our erstwhile ally is not confined within its boundaries. May I read to you a few words from a document recently come into my hands?'

The judge waved a weary hand. 'Oh, very well; you have my permission, in the fond hope that it may have some bearing on the matter in hand.'

'Thank you, your honour.' Featherby took up a dog-eared pamphlet from the pile of papers before him. '"This Revolution",' he quoted in a voice heavy with melodrama, '"is not the Revolution of Marat or the Revolution of Robespierre. It is not the Revolution of the Girondists, nor of the Jacobins. It is the Revolution of the people. And it is a universal Revolution; a Revolution without borders. No power on earth and no combination of national governments, though backed by military might, can resist its inevitable spread to every land where the will of the people is not sovereign."'

He let fall the tattered document as though it were infected with the germs of some fatal plague. 'This seditious broadside, your honour, is the work, not of a French rabble-rouser, but of a British radical press, one with which the prisoner is very familiar. The man Keene is an apostle of darkness, newly come from England.' He stressed and savoured the last word brandishing it as a red rag to his ex-colonial audience, who responded with murmurs of outrage and shouted oaths. With impeccable timing the lawyer moved to his peroration. 'This man is wanted by the government of his own country for capital crimes and he has come among us intent on spreading his pernicious gospel of so-called liberty.'

Keene stared at the public benches and felt the hair at the back of his neck bristle. He saw a crowd of sober citizens in the process of being transmuted into a mob by Featherby's oratory. It was a sight the like of which he had witnessed before – several times in Paris and once in London, where the militia had been sent in to disperse a crowd at sabre-point, leaving a public square strewn with dead and dying. There was always a moment, a temporal fulcrum, when a herd instinct of rage took over, and Keene sensed that that moment was about to come. A few more of the lawyer's flammatory phrases and these Delawarians would rise in their places ready to tear him limb from limb.

The only person immune from the effects of Featherby's ranting was the judge. He now poured cold water on the emotional coals. 'And exactly what are the illegal acts or words for which you have brought the prisoner into my court? I trust I need not remind you that sedition is defined as incitement of others, by means of deeds, writings or speech, to undermine the constitution or those charged with upholding the constitution. In what ways has Mr Keene, in your submission, contravened the sedition laws?'

Featherby held up a sheaf of papers. 'I have sworn affidavits for your honour stating that the prisoner publicly advocated what he called the "people's revolution", which includes the abolition of private property and the removal from office of any who oppose the will of the people – whatever that might be,' he added with a sneer.

Silently the judge extended his hand. Featherby crossed to the desk and placed his evidence upon it. Several minutes passed while the judge read the material before him. The murmurings on the public benches gradually subsided and an atmosphere of expectant stillness settled on the room. Keene waited tensely for the verdict. His plan to become a figure of notoriety among the good people of Dover had succeeded more rapidly than he could have imagined, but had it worked too well? If the judge, who clearly had no great affection for Featherby, dismissed his demand for a full trial, Keene's standing among the radical element in the town would be established and he might well expect an approach from the leaders of the republican underground. But if the sharp-tongued official decided that there was a case to be answered, then he might be detained for days, weeks or even months. In that situation would Hamilton be able to extract him? He thought of the meticulous minister concerned above all else with his own standing in the government and knew that he would do nothing to risk his position. No, the agent of powerful men was, as always, on his own. He was suddenly aware that his name was being called.

'Mr Keene,' said the judge, 'how long have you been in Dover?'

'Two days, your honour.'

'And in that brief time have you addressed or attempted to convene any public meetings?'

'Hardly, your honour. One of those days was spent in your prison.'

'Just so, just so.' The judge nodded and turned to Featherby. 'These statements all refer to the same incident, do they not?'

The lawyer nodded.

'A private discussion involving Mr Keene and half a dozen of our own citizens.'

'Prominent citizens of excellent standing, your honour.'

'Their probity is not in question, sir, nor is it relevant. The substantive point is that this was a private discussion.'

'It was in a public place, your honour. The prisoner was

quite shameless in giving loud expression to his seditious opinions. Others would certainly have heard him.'

'Is it, then, your submission that people who chance to overhear a private conversation in a drinking house are guilty of gathering together as a seditious assembly?'

Featherby avoided the trap. 'It is my submission that a man who is wanted for capital offences in his own country and who, within hours of his arrival in our town, openly voices dangerous opinions is a menace to our society.'

'Hmm!' The judge put his hands together and rested his chin upon them. When he spoke it was quietly, almost to himself. 'By that criterion, sir, many of our founding fathers would have suffered the full rigour of the law. They were men at odds with their own governments in England, France, the Low Countries; men with very definite ideas about freedom and justice.'

'May I respectfully point out, your honour, that the cases are not comparable. The original settlers came to create a new society, not to overturn an existing one. We continue to welcome hundreds of emigrants into our midst. Even now many men and their families are fleeing to our shores from the slave insurrection in St Domingue. We willingly provide them with refuge. All we ask of them is that they obey our laws and uphold our constitution. Unfortunately, some of the people who come here have other motives. We must be vigilant in weeding out subversives if we are to protect those very laws and freedoms our founders came to establish.'

There was chorus of 'Ayes!' and 'Hear hims!' from the body of the courtroom. The judge surveyed with a weary frown the rows of angry faces.

'One of those freedoms,' he pointed out, 'is freedom of speech. It's enshrined in the constitution which I am sworn to uphold.'

Keene watched the contest closely and pondered where the power really lay. In the law, as represented by the judge? In the politicians – for the game Featherby was playing was politics, pure and simple? In the people – which really meant those fears, prejudices and ambitions with which a community buttresses itself against the storms of new and challenging ideas? The lawyer's next words removed from his mind any doubts he had on that score.

'This morning,' Featherby said, in a quiet, matter-of-fact voice, 'I was in conversation with the governor.'

Keene saw the almost imperceptible flicker of the judge's eyelids.

'He is resolved that no toehold should be given to anarchy in the territory under his jurisdiction; that Delaware should maintain its proud tradition of being the staunchest supporter of the federal constitution. Under that constitution the people are sovereign. I ask, in his name, that we let a jury of the honest citizens of Dover decide in the case of the State versus Keene.' The lawyer sat down and the public cheered him.

Moments later Keene was on his way back to the cells.

Six

K eene spent the next three days out of contact with the world. Now he was really alone, oppressively alone. He was allowed out of his cell once in every twenty-four hours to empty the bucket provided for his easement and to walk for thirty minutes in an enclosed courtyard. Even there he took his exercise in solitude. If there were other prisoners in the jail – and he knew that there must be – he was deprived of their company. Or it would probably be truer to say that they were deprived of his company. The authorities presumably feared that the Englishman would infect any other human being with whom he came in contact with some deadly ideological contagion. Twice daily the jailer brought his ration of meagre prison fare, and he, it seemed, had taken a vow of silence, under strict orders to avoid infection. Always he hurried in, set down the bowl of food, collected the empty container and withdrew hastily. When Keene spoke he turned his head sharply away. Every question or comment met with the same response. Keene asked if he might have some books or if he might know the date of his trial. He remarked that the food was too hot or too cold or too salty or not salty enough. Nothing shook the jailer out of his role as deaf mute.

Keene's mood passed rapidly from anger to brooding resentment. He felt the ultimate humiliation of complete helplessness. He was powerless to do or say or think anything that would change his current situation or make any preparation for future events. He was completely at the mercy of other men, who would do with him what

61

they wanted, when they wanted. This humour in its turn
went away – or, rather, he thrust it aside. He would not
let Featherby and his witch-hunting accomplices force him
into despair. He would find a way out of his predicament.

He crafted a plan. First he would have to overpower the
guard. That would not be difficult; the man was overweight
and sluggish. But what then? How many other guards were
there in the building? And could he find his way out? Keene
drifted into slumber on the third night with his problems
unresolved.

He was roughly shaken into wakefulness to find a light
being swung before his bleary eyes. As he struggled into
a sitting position rough hands grasped his arms. He was
yanked to his feet and marched from the cell. Keene's
rescuers were four men, all masked, one of whom carried a
closed lantern. They hurried him along corridors to an outer
door, without even a whispered word. The escape from the
building took less than a minute and Keene noticed that at no
point did they encounter a guard or any kind of obstruction.
Doors were open and keyless and no lights glimmered in
any of the windows. He had no chance to reflect on this.
In the courtyard the four men mounted waiting horses and
Keene was pulled up behind one of them.

The journey, through streets black and without feature
in the moonless night, took the party out of the town.
Even in the open countryside no words passed between
Keene's companions. But he did not have long to wait for
explanations. After ten minutes or so they came to a cluster
of farm buildings. One of the men dismounted and opened
a barn door, which was closed again as soon as everyone
had entered. Now lamps were lit and, as he jumped to the
ground, Keene was able to take stock of his surroundings.
The barn was a large one and well stacked with this season's
hay. The horses were tethered and left to munch contentedly
on fodder while Keene was roughly pushed towards the far
end of the building.

'Gentlemen, I thank . . . '

'Hold your tongue! Sit down over there!' Keene felt a heavy hand in the small of his back and knew that his 'deliverance' was not what it had at first seemed.

He was pushed towards a rough kitchen chair and forced down on to it. He struggled to resist but was powerless against the two muscular men who held him while a third strapped his arms and legs to the chair frame. They stepped away and stood in a semicircle, smirking down at him. Keene stared back. He saw rough-looking countrymen in coats of heavy cloth and hats pulled down over faces which remained masked.

'Mr Keene, welcome to your trial.' The leader of the group, clad more expensively in a black tailcoat of English cut over well-polished boots, stepped out of the shadows, removing his gauntlets. Like his companions, his upper face was concealed by a dark hood into which eyeholes had been cut. But Keene identified him as soon as he spoke.

'Mr Featherby, we meet again.'

Instantly he felt the lash of the lawyer's leather glove across his cheek.

'Trial rule number one: no names – except the prisoner's.'

'Trial?' Keene's sense of outrage was stronger than his foreboding about his imminent fate. 'Where does all this fit into the American pattern of justice . . . Mr Featherby?'

The gauntlet cut across the other side of Keene's face.

'We've no time for your insolence.' Featherby glanced at one of his companions. 'Read the indictment.'

The man pulled a crumpled piece of paper from his pocket. He cleared his throat and read in a husky voice. 'Treason against the people of the State of Delaware.'

The Englishman laughed. '"Treason"? A fine catch-all word.' He glowered at the lawyer and noticed the trickle of spittle from one corner of his mouth. 'Whatever your murderous purpose, get on with it! Drop all this legal mummery and be damned!'

Featherby nodded to one of his accomplices, a barrel-chested man with the build of a blacksmith. This giant swung his fist so hard at Keene's jaw that the chair was flung backwards. The prisoner's head still reeled from the blow as Featherby's cronies lifted the chair back into place.

The glint in Featherby's eyes showed that he enjoyed the brutality but he continued in a voice stripped of emotion. 'The evidence,' he demanded.

Another member of the group took a step forward. 'The prisoner said in my hearing that France is leading the way in popular insurrection and he had come to help spread it in America.' The words were a well-learned recitation rather than a statement.

The tall man nodded and looked around at his companions and pronounced solemnly, 'Members of the jury, you have heard the evidence against the prisoner. Do you find him guilty or not guilty?'

'Guilty.' The word fell in unison from three pairs of lips.

Keene glared up at them. 'My God, Featherby, what sort of a farce is this? You're supposed to be a man of law, not judge, jury and prosecutor in a mockery of everything law exists to defend.'

'Silence! You will talk only if and when the court permits.'

'Oh, go ahead, play your games,' Keene retorted. 'I'm not taking any part in them.'

The lawyer held up a hand in a solemn gesture, as though he were taking an oath. 'The sentence of this court is that you be removed from hence and hanged until you be dead, and may the Lord have mercy on your soul.'

Keene laughed contemptuously. 'At least the French Revolutionaries you so much despise put on a decent show before they send people to the guillotine. They believe that justice that is not public is not worthy the name.'

'You would be wise not to provoke me further, Mr Keene.' Featherby waved his gauntlet menacingly. 'I have the power of life and death over you.'

'Really? I thought that decision had already been taken.'

'The court has authority, under exceptional circumstances, to commute sentence.'

Keene nodded and smiled. 'Ah, now I see what this is all about: you want information.'

Featherby did not answer immediately. He turned to the 'blacksmith'. 'Make ready,' he ordered.

Keene and his captors watched as the man went across to the horses, unfastened a coil of rope from one of the saddles and, with well-practised aim, threw one end over one of the cross beams supporting the roof. With a matter-of-fact air he adjusted the height of the dangling noose, then fastened the other end to a cleat on the barn wall.

Keene stared at the oval shape swaying in the draughts that filtered through the building. Until that moment the bizarre unreality of the nocturnal pantomime had numbed his emotions. Now fear broke through the absurdity. He was plunged gasping into the icy certainty that these self-appointed guardians of the state would kill him – in cold blood and without a qualm. Why? Because they were fanatics able to clothe their own bestial instincts in the shabby trappings of pseudo-law. But also because his own subterfuge had been too successful. He had posed as a dangerous radical and these mindless reactionaries had taken him at face value. Was it too late to point out their mistake? Probably. Yet somehow he must try to calm his thudding heartbeats and make Featherby listen to the truth.

The lawyer was speaking again. 'Mr Keene, this tribunal goes by the name of the Regulators. It exists to make good those deficiencies which, unfortunately, exist in the state's legal system. Ours is a young and vulnerable society. The constitution we have so painstakingly constructed is constantly under attack by subversive elements like you, men who are clever enough to use against the common good those very safeguards we have built into the system to guarantee the freedoms of our citizens. We cannot allow everything we have worked for to be eaten away from within—'

Keene saw his opportunity. 'You are absolutely right,' he interrupted. 'That's why I have been sent here by the federal government to infiltrate the organisation of the republican dissidents.'

That statement brought snorts of laughter from his captors. Featherby said, 'Don't insult the court with such pathetic lies. If you want to save your miserable life tell us all you know about Edmond Genet's network.'

'I'm employed by Alexander Hamilton precisely for the purpose of gathering information about that network.' Even as he spoke the words Keene knew how unconvincing they sounded.

Featherby turned abruptly. 'Untie him and bring him,' he said curtly.

The other two men released their prisoner from the chair and marched him, one to each arm, towards the execution area. Keene went limp, stumbling like one in the grip of terror. Then, with a sudden jerk, he broke free and raced towards the large barn doors. Ignoring the shouts behind him, he grasped the wooden bar which rested in iron sockets. It was a tight fit. Just as the beam clattered to the ground a heavy hand fell on his shoulder and spun him round. For the second time he felt the force of the 'blacksmith's' massive fist. He collapsed, almost unconscious.

'Close it!' Featherby called from the other end of the barn. 'We don't want to attract any attention.'

The Englishman was half dragged to where the chair now stood beneath the swinging noose. His hands were tied behind his back and strong arms hoisted him on to the seat, where he stood swaying slightly and trying to pull his mind into focus.

'One last chance, Mr Keene. Full details of the French operation and we'll set you on a boat back to Europe.'

Slowly, too slowly, the swirling mists inside Keene's head cleared. 'Look, don't you think you'd better check with Mr Hamilton?' he said. 'If you only discover your mistake after you've killed me the consequences could be very serious.' He looked down at the lawyer and saw the first sign of hesitation.

There was a long pause in the proceedings. The other Regulators looked to Featherby, who stood flapping his gloves against his thigh.

What broke the tension was the last thing Keene expected. There was a swishing sound overhead. Then another. As Keene looked up the noise repeated itself and he saw a bright light streak through the air and embed itself in the piled hay. Immediately the dry material burst into flame. Other fires had already been started by the buzzing projectiles. From a doorway in the wall to his left a voice shouted, 'Keene! This way! Quickly!'

Keene jumped down from the chair. As he did so the 'blacksmith' lunged towards him. A pistol shot rang out and the burly American fell to the ground, screaming and clutching his leg. Keene's other captors were in total confusion. More burning arrows rained down on the hay and flames were already grasping the timbers. The horses reared and whinnied in terror. Featherby screamed, 'Stop Keene!' but his minions were too intent on saving themselves to bother with the prisoner. One tried to unhitch the horses and was sent sprawling by a flailing hoof. The other ran to the far end of the barn where there was no conflagration and wrestled with the large wagon doors.

Keene sprinted awkwardly towards the side entrance, his hands still strapped behind him. Someone grabbed him, pulled him through the doorway and immediately closed it. He was vaguely aware of someone else pushing a heavy object up against the door.

There seemed to be several people in the farmyard, some on foot, some on horseback.

'Hold still,' a sharp voice ordered. Keene felt his bonds deftly sliced through.

'Come on! There's a horse here!'

Another dark figure gave him a leg up into the saddle.

Lurid light splashed suddenly over the scene as flames

broke through part of the barn wall. Behind him Keene heard cries and the sound of fists hammering on the door. 'Are you going to leave them in there?' he shouted.

'They'll find a way out . . . Or perhaps they won't.' Keene recognised the voice as that of the quiet bookseller, John Bowman.

Then, for the second time that night, he cantered off into the darkness with a company of men he did not know.

This time the journey ended in the stable yard of a substantial house on the outskirts of Dover. Here the group dispersed, most members going, Keene assumed, to their own homes. The leader, whom he now recognised as the man called Jensen, led the way through a back door and a succession of domestic offices to a well-appointed salon where they were joined, moments later, by Bowman. Jensen spoke briefly to a liveried servant then waved Keene to a bergère chair close to the hearth in which a lively fire burned. He removed his own topcoat and flung it nonchalantly over the back of a delicate-looking sofa covered in pink silk. He poured brandy from a decanter standing on a small side table and handed glasses to the others. Then he threw his bulk down on the sofa so heavily that Keene thought the slender cabriole legs must buckle.

'Well, that was a lively night's work!' The words emerged through a fleshy mouth stretched in a wide smile. 'Here's to your resurrection, Mr Keene.' Jensen raised his brimming glass, then downed the contents at a gulp.

'What can I say?' the Englishman responded. 'Thank you, sir, for saving my life.'

'Thank John. It was he who insisted that your hide was worth rescuing. For my part, I'm not utterly convinced.'

Bowman smiled sheepishly. 'Our conversation in jail indicated that we shared the same ideas about liberty.'

'I didn't realise you were an activist in the cause.'

Bowman shook his head. 'I wasn't. Too much the book-worm, the student of ideas. My eyes saw nothing but lines of print when they should have been watching the rise to power of Featherby and his ilk.'

Keene looked at the young man, an innocent caught up now in affairs whose complexity he could not understand. 'You've put your life in danger on my account.'

'No, I was a marked man before you came into my shop. Then, when I walked free from the court . . . Well, Featherby was furious. His men had already ransacked the shop. When I went back there the place was a shambles – books scattered around and torn apart; my desk ransacked; papers missing. I stood there looking at the wreck and felt sick. But only for a few moments. Suddenly –' Bowman stared into the fire – 'it was like a vision, an *Aufklärung*, an enlightenment. The Regulators had set me free. They had destroyed my past life for me. It no longer shackled me. Instead of just thinking, dreaming about those things I believed in, there was nothing to stop me working for them, fighting for them. I just walked away from the shop. I haven't been back.'

At that moment the door opened to admit a corpulent little man, elegant from the buckles of his court shoes to the top of his powdered peruke. The others stood as he crossed the floor with a languid stride. From the pocket of his green-braided waistcoat he took a pair of spectacles and peered at Keene. 'Mission accomplished, *n'est ce pas*?' he remarked nonchalantly.

Jensen inclined his head respectfully. 'Yes, your Excellency, and in the nick of time. I have the honour to present Mr George Keene. Mr Keene, may I introduce M. Auguste Belmont, consular representative of the People's Republic of France?'

'Welcome, Mr Keene,' the consul said, seating himself. 'You seem to have crammed a great deal into your brief stay in Dover.' He turned to Jensen. 'Tell me about the night's events.'

'It was partly luck and partly good organisation. Vincent was watching Featherby's house but he almost lost him. The slippery snake went out the back way. As soon as he rendezvoused with Bates, Ormond and McDonald at the

69

courthouse, he knew what was afoot and came to rouse
me and the others. I guessed they would be headed for
Ford's farm. Featherby has some kind of a hold over old
man Ford. He uses the place for his nocturnal gatherings
and no questions asked.'

'And there you found Mr Keene?' Belmont asked. 'What
did those *canailles* do to you, sir?'

Keene gave an account of his experiences at the farm.

When he had finished the Frenchman nodded vigorously.
'Yes, they are of the same feather as the old royalist vultures
in France. They make and execute their own laws to keep
themselves and their kind in power. Well, this time we have
thwarted them.'

'What happens now?' Keene asked. 'If Featherby is
dead . . .'

Bowman sighed. 'I wouldn't wager on that. The devil
protects his own.'

'Then he'll have men out looking for me.'

'I don't think so, Mr Keene,' Jensen said. 'He won't want
to see you back in court giving your version of this night's
events.'

'Then perhaps I should take the initiative; go to the judge
and expose Featherby.'

The other men exchanged glances. Belmont spoke for
them. 'That would draw attention to the activities of our
friends and we would rather that did not happen. Anyway,
you can be more use to the cause elsewhere.'

'I can? Tell me how.' Keene's whole body was weary
from his recent exertions and his jaw throbbed with pain.
He wanted nothing more than a soft bed and several hours
of oblivion. But he forced himself to display eagerness.

Belmont leaned forward, his pale blue eyes peering
intently through the lenses. 'What is your honest assessment
of the situation here in America, Mr Keene?'

The answer came readily because the Englishman had
tutored himself well. 'The people's revolution, which ulti-
mately is inevitable, made a good start and powered the

breakaway from royalist imperialism. Unfortunately, the movement fell into the hands of a mercantile-political caucus whose only interest is keeping power in their own hands. Most of the men now running state and national legislatures are the same men who held office under the old regime. They are as intent on suppressing the aspirations of the people as were their masters in London.'

Belmont's solemn nod indicated that so far he was satisfied. 'When you were in Philadelphia, what impression did you form of the party divisions at the political centre?' he asked.

'Hamilton is a haughty, self-loving petty-aristo with a passion for all things British. He would be nothing loth to setting up a monarchy.'

'And Jefferson?'

'A true republican, but his position has become weakened by the war between France and Britain. As long as America remains shackled to England by the bonds of trade his wealthier supporters will resist coming out on the side of the people.'

Belmont sighed. 'Hamilton has had his lackey, Chief Justice Jay, draft a declaration of neutrality, and Washington – the great general – is inclined to it.'

'The President no longer speaks for the people on that matter,' Bowman interposed. 'There's widespread sympathy for the common folk of France.'

Belmont slapped a hand against his well-fleshed knee. 'Exactly! That's why we must take action *le plus fort*, rapid and vigorous. All is in the balance. The citizens must be mobilised. They must make their voice heard. They must sway Congress. Force the executive to act. For this we need every man. Are you with us, Mr Keene?'

'What do you want of me?' Keene asked quietly.

The consul motioned to Jensen. 'Gabriel, outline the plan for our friend while I recharge the glasses.'

'You're sure, Citizen?' Keene was aware that the pugilistic Jensen had been scrutinising him closely ever since they

71

had entered the room. He sensed that Belmont's henchman was not entirely convinced that this untried Englishman was to be trusted with secrets. 'I have many contacts among the radical clubs in Britain,' he said. 'The only man with the name of "Keene" that they know of is dead.'

'Good. I'm delighted to hear it.' Keene accepted the cognac his host handed him. Languidly he sipped the excellent spirit while his brain whirled. 'I only wish the Westminster stipendiary magistrates shared that view.'

'Perhaps you'd expand on that enigmatic statement for us.'

Keene improvised, weaving together fact and invention. 'Your sources doubtless informed you that George Keene was deported to Australia with several other brave fellows aboard HMS *Spry*, a vessel which was subsequently lost at sea.'

Jensen nodded almost imperceptibly.

'Fortunately, George Keene was not aboard the doomed vessel when she sailed. Friends engineered my escape en route to the port and concealed me in London.'

'And the authorities knew nothing of this?'

'The mud-brained squirearchy in Norfolk where I was apprehended preferred to cover up their incompetence. Their counterparts in London were less accommodating.' Keene paused and watched his audience over the rim of his glass. The three men were listening intently. 'You are, of course, aware of the infamous Police Act, passed last year, which introduced a body of paid magistrates answerable directly to the Crown and not to parliament. It is a system copied directly from the royalist secret police in France and it took the new snoopers very little time to set up their own similar network of spies and informers. They sniffed out George Keene, and I was obliged to slip across the Channel for a few months.'

Bowman looked up sharply. 'You were in France? You've never mentioned that.'

Keene thought quickly. 'You must forgive me, John; I've

learned to be circumspect about my relationships with the leaders of the Revolution.' He saw the consul raise his eyebrows and hurried on before Belmont could test him out with detailed questions. 'Yes, I spent some weeks in Paris in the summer,' he laughed, 'moving from the fox's lair to the huntsman's kennels.'

'That's an odd riddle,' Jensen grunted.

'What I mean is that I made the acquaintance of Citizen Inspector Dossonville, the Chief of Police. I was able to provide him with useful information about English spies working for the monarchist alliance.'

Belmont smiled. 'Dear Jean-Baptiste; such a clever man. All he lacks is a good tailor. Did you not find him something of a sloven?'

Keene spotted the trap. 'Indeed, no, he seemed a well-turned out gentleman and keeps an excellent table. As to guile, well, it was a relief to discover that the Revolution has men like him, capable of outwitting Pitt's lumbering bloodhounds at every turn.'

Belmont stood suddenly. He crossed to Keene and slapped him on the shoulder. 'Well, Mr Keene, I am delighted that our friends here were able to save you from a lynching. Your death would have been a sad loss to our cause. Welcome to the friends of liberty. Gabriel, explain our strategy . . . '

Jensen lumbered to his feet. 'Citizen, a word.' He drew Belmont to the other end of the room.

Keene watched with apparent nonchalance as the two men engaged in a whispered conversation. It rapidly became clear that the surly American was making no impression on his superior. Belmont several times shook his head vigorously and finally turned away with a curt, '*Voilà tout!*'

When he had resumed his seat he began a businesslike exposition of his plans. 'We have to mobilise the American people, inspire them to exercise their sovereignty, show them they don't have to surrender it to a government hundreds of miles away in Philadelphia, made up of men who only have their own interests at heart. To that end

Citizen Genet is about to embark on a campaign of public meetings which will take him all along the coast, speaking in strategically selected towns.'

Keene nodded. 'From what I have seen and heard of the chargé d'affaires, he is very persuasive.'

'He is an excellent advocate of the people's cause. Our task is to prepare the way for him. That is where you can serve most effectively – you and John Bowman here.'

'I'm a stranger . . . '

'But you know what the enemies of freedom are capable of. You can witness to the fact that both in England and America the lackeys of monarchist repression will stop at nothing to cling on to their power and privileges. Gabriel, tell our friend what we have in mind.'

With ill-concealed reluctance Jensen obliged. 'We go on ahead and link up with our local activists. We organise small preparatory meetings in coffee houses, inns, people's homes. We ensure a good audience for Citizen Genet. Immediately after his talk we collect names on a petition to Congress and organise whatever other coordinated action may be necessary.'

'Such as?' Keene pressed.

Jensen scowled. 'That's all you need know for now.'

Minutes later the party dispersed. Jensen left, scooping up his topcoat and stalking from the room with the briefest of nods to Belmont. Keene and Bowman were shown to chambers prepared for them and the Englishman was glad to strip off his clothes and drop wearily on to the bed. His limbs were tired, his jaw ached and his head throbbed. But what kept sleep at bay until the verge of dawn was the knowledge that he was betraying good men.

Seven

'S o I say to you, my friends, revive the spirit of '76! Finish the work nobly begun! Fashion the new world for which your fathers, sons and brothers died!' The orator's voice climbed steadily in a crescendo. 'Did they die in vain? Have you forgotten Briar's Creek and Hobkirk Hill and Cowpens and King's Mount?'

'No! No!' The shouts came from men Keene had planted at the back of the crowd and were taken up by a hundred voices till they merged into a roar that Edmond Genet had to calm by raising both hands in the air.

'My friends, I never doubted you, nor did the people of France, who stood shoulder to shoulder with you in your historic struggle. Now it is they who hold high the standard of liberty. Encircled by the forces of a decaying tyranny, facing enemies within and without, they look to you for support. I see from your faces that they do not look in vain.'

While most of the audience cheered and applauded, the plenipotentiary of Republican France raised a glass of wine to his lips and made the simple act of refreshment look like a salute to the four hundred citizens of Charleston filling the auditorium of the Dock Street theatre. It was the fifth time Keene had witnessed this seemingly spontaneous gesture; the fifth time he had heard the speech delivered almost word for word from platforms in Richmond, Norfolk, Fayetteville, Wilmington and now here in the major port and one-time capital of South Carolina. There was no denying that the man was good. For these occasions he dressed simply – no

75

wig, a brown coat with little braiding over a cream waistcoat, and trousers, the warm, casual garment favoured by many Americans. He bustled energetically about the stage, his address well committed to memory.

The Frenchman was excellently briefed by the small suite of activists with which he travelled. They kept him informed of those local issues which inspired feelings of pride or resentment and Genet played these aces with the skill of a fairground mountebank. Thus, in his speech to the good citizens of Charleston he had been sure to make several references to the devastating English siege which had so damaged the town and wounded the pride of its inhabitants in 1780. There was a large residue of anti-British feeling here but was it sufficient for the Charlestonians to want to embroil themselves in a foreign war? The mercantile community here – always conservative – was large and powerful. Keene could see groups of them in the audience; rocks of scepticism around which the excitement of their neighbours crashed and eddied, leaving them unmoved.

From his vantage point he gazed out over the rows of seats facing the stage. The platform was filled with what was supposed to be an impressive display of prominent citizens eager for the republican cause. They occupied three rows of chairs behind the speaker's reading stand and Keene sat at the end of the back row. Throughout Genet's forty-five minute tirade he watched the reactions of the listeners. Everything had gone very much according to plan in the earlier meetings. Genet's revolutionary fervour had been cheered to the echo, leading politicians including three congressmen had pledged their support to the anti-neutrality campaign and hundreds of signatures had been secured for the movement's petition.

But there was a different feel about the Charleston gathering. The displays of enthusiasm were confined to areas of the auditorium. The listeners outside these 'patches' sat in silence or held there own muffled conversations. Could it be that the Federalist opposition was better organised in this town or were there genuine local issues that Genet's researchers had failed to detect?

His mind went back over the three weeks that he had been part of the Frenchman's travelling circus. Day had followed hectic day and the scores of people he had met blurred into a confusion of lamplit faces. Many of the radical groups he had encountered had gathered after dark in shuttered rooms, in barns and outhouses, secrecy adding a frisson of excitement to their fervour. Anger, passion, conviction, hope – he read them all in the eyes of these ordinary Americans and recognised the emotions because he had seen them before. They had confronted him in the anxious glances of Norfolk farmworkers when the clatter of King George's troops was suddenly heard on the cobbles outside. They had glowed in the exultant vengeance of sans-culottes in the Place du Carousel.

To all these Revolutionary cells Keene and his companions had brought the encouraging revelation that they were not alone; that they were part of an irresistible tidal wave of *real* democracy – rule, as Rousseau defined it, in the name and for the benefit of that great body of ordinary men and women from whom all power derives. The clandestine planning sessions had gone well. The zealots had sallied forth and drawn their friends and neighbours – the cautious, the half-committed and the merely curious – to hear the Frenchman tell stirring tales of the brave deeds done by his countrymen in the van of the battle for universal brotherhood and freedom. And after the meetings, when he could organise some time alone, Keene had hastily written his reports – names, addresses, meeting places – and despatched them to Philadelphia by special couriers waiting at pre-arranged locations.

Here in Charleston, however, things were different. Here opinions were not clearly clothed in the black and white of rival ideologies but in the drab and confusing greys of reality. Anti-British feeling certainly ran deep but it was not necessarily accompanied by an enthusiasm for extremist politics and all things French.

Keene sensed trouble. Instinctively he knew that it would be wise to draw a swift end to the meeting. From his pocket he pulled a pencil and a scrap of paper. 'Don't call for questions', he scribbled, and he passed the note to the man in front. He watched as it made its way towards the speaker. It reached Jensen, seated in the centre of the front row, and Keene saw the large head with its long, tangled cascade of dark hair bend over the message. He saw Jensen hold a brief, whispered conversation with his neighbour, then turn to glance in his direction. A scowl spread over the man's heavy features. He stuffed the paper into his pocket.

Genet was into his final peroration. 'My friends, our movement – the movement of *real* republicanism – is growing in all parts of your great country. It is growing among the leaders in the state legislatures and in Congress. It is growing among the nation's thinkers and philosophers. It is growing among the men of action who expelled the British and who know that the war is yet but half won. But, most important of all, my friends, it is growing in the hearts of the people – the farmers and shopkeepers, the cobblers and weavers, the fathers and mothers determined to pass to their children an inheritance of LIBERTY! A liberty that exists in more than name, that is not limited, that is not measured out to them by the rich and powerful. A liberty that is theirs by right.' He paused and strode to the very front of the stage. He held out his hands to the audience in a gesture of combined benediction and supplication. 'I see before me the brave citizens of Charleston. There is not one among you who has not already endured much to win the true liberty. Will you draw back now that the prize is almost within your grasp?' He paused while the planted supporters led a cry of 'No!' 'Will Charleston take a lead in the great crusade?' As less than half the audience chorused 'Yes!' Citizen Genet resumed his seat.

The platform party dutifully stood to give the speaker his

ovation. They were joined by perhaps a third of the audience. Before the applause could subside of its own accord, the chairman, Charleston's deputy governor, called for silence. His excellency, he intimated, would now be happy to take questions. Keene groaned.

A tall man in the front row jumped to his feet. 'Your governors have set free the rabble of rebellious blacks in the West Indies. Is that your idea of liberty?'

Genet rose all smiles. 'There has been a deal of exaggeration about affairs in our Caribbean settlements . . . '

'Exaggeration!' the protester screamed. 'Don't you dare accuse me of exaggeration, sir! The black savages came pouring into my plantation. They slaughtered my manager and his wife. I was forced to flee with my family. We arrived here with nothing but the clothes we stood up in.' He turned to face the rows behind him. 'And we weren't alone, as everyone here knows. Thousands of us on Saint Domingue have been dispossessed, ruined. We've lost everything we've worked for, that our fathers have worked for.'

Others were now on their feet, shouting their support. From somewhere in the middle of the auditorium a voice rose above the rest. 'And when we complained, what did Genet's fine revolutionary government do about it?'

Genet struggled to make himself heard amidst the furore. 'The black population seized their own freedom . . . '

'No thanks to the French!'

'What aid did they send? Nothing! Not one ship! Not one soldier! Not so much as a tattered tricolour!'

'They handed our land and our homes over to savages!'

The chairman made a belated attempt to regain control of the meeting. 'Gentlemen, gentlemen, calm yourselves! This is not what we are here . . . '

Now the republican element found its voice. 'Liberty's for all, not just white men!' The cry from the back of the theatre was taken up as a chant by other voices. 'Liberty for all! Liberty for all!'

Back came the angry responses.

'Nigger-lovers!'

'Damned anarchists!'

Within seconds men were throwing punches, clambering over seats, grappling in the aisles, rolling on the floor. A group of protesters made a rush for the stage.

All this time Genet had been standing as one stupefied, surveying the riot. Those around him seemed equally transfixed. Keene ran forward and grabbed the plenipotentiary by the arm. 'This way, sir!' he yelled. 'In God's name, stir yourself!'

Others now clustered round the Frenchman. They hustled him to the rear of the platform, out through the side curtains, stumbling over backstage obstacles in the semi-gloom, until they reached a door giving on to the street. They found themselves in what was little more than a garbage-strewn alleyway between buildings.

Jensen assumed command. 'We must get Citizen Genet back to his hotel,' he shouted, and, turning right, he strode briskly towards the centre of the town. The others followed like bewildered sheep. They had gone no more than a few paces when a group of angry men came round the corner ahead of them, brandishing sticks and pistols. 'There he is!' someone shouted, and the mob broke into a run.

Keene and his companions turned abruptly, getting in each others way as they stumbled towards the far end of the lane. Keene found himself next to Genet as they emerged into a broad street of warehouses close to the waterfront.

The Frenchman was red in the face and clutching his chest. 'Mon Dieu! Impossible!' he wheezed. 'My heart!'

Keene grabbed his elbow and steered him straight across the thoroughfare. Suddenly Genet fell to his knees. 'Save yourselves,' he panted. 'I cannot . . . '

Keene hauled him bodily to his feet and half-dragged, half-carried him towards the buildings opposite. They dived in front of a wagon. The horse reared in alarm and the driver cursed loudly. The moment's confusion gained them precious time. Their pursuers, who were almost upon them, were hindered by the wagoner's struggle to get his animal under control.

Jensen had reached the far side. He turned. 'For God's sake, keep moving! This way,' he yelled, pointing to a gap between the warehouses.

'Genet's ill,' Keene said. 'He can't go on!'

Jensen glanced quickly at the trembling Frenchman. 'Leave him, then. He's the one they want.' He turned and raced down the alley. The other members of the party were already running in that direction.

Suddenly Bowman appeared at Keene's side. 'Come on!' he shouted and took Genet's other arm.

For a few yards they followed their retreating colleagues. They squeezed past a cart unloading sacks of grain which were being winched aloft to the upper storey of the storehouse on their right. Immediately beyond, Keene spotted an open door. 'This way,' he called and hauled the limp burden through. Inside he and Bowman let Genet collapse onto a pile of empty sacks. They leaped into the shadow beside the doorway as the shrieking posse rushed past.

As soon as all was quiet Bowman knelt beside the stricken man and loosened his clothing. Genet lay very still, moaning faintly, his eyelids flickering. 'His breathing is very heavy,' Bowman said. 'We ought to get him to a doctor.'

Keene was sceptical. The foppish Frenchman was very young to be having trouble with his heart. He had seen plenty of sick people in his time. He had also observed men rendered immobile by cowardly panic. Which category did Genet fit into? He had his suspicions.

They were no longer alone. A little group of warehouse workers had gathered round and Keene turned to explain the situation to them. 'A friend of ours has been taken ill suddenly. He needs a physician. Is there one nearby?'

'Not in this part of town as I know of,' one of the men ventured.

Another agreed. 'Only chandlers and customs officers around here. You want White Point. Lots of quacks there. More money to be made out of treating rich folks than the likes of us.' He spat expertly on the dusty floor.

A third took a step forward, peering inquisitively. 'Foreigner, is he?'

Keene nodded. 'French.'

'Oh well, there's your answer, then,' the man said.

'What do you mean?'

'There's a couple of Frenchie ships in the harbour. One of 'em may have a doctor aboard.'

Keene glanced at Bowman. 'That may be our best option, John. Can you look after Genet while I go in search of someone who can do something for him?'

'I guess so.' Bowman looked up. 'But be quick. He looks really sick to me.'

Charleston's roadstead was thick with shipping. From the quayside Keene looked out on an interlacing of bare masts and rigging with, here and there, the flags of several nations flashing garish colours like brilliant butterflies caught in a web. He strode the length of the bustling quay, looking for the tricolour. So absorbed was he in his search that he did not notice until he approached the seaward end of the harbour wall that people all around were clambering to vantage points and gazing out beyond the anchorage. Only when he recognised a different sound above the trundling of carts and the squeal of ships' windlasses did he realise what was exciting everyone. There was no mistaking the thudding of distant cannon fire.

Keene paused to help a fishwife who was clambering up on to a wagon. 'Who's fighting who?' he asked.

The woman smirked down at him. 'Another British prize being brought in by privateers, I shouldn't wonder. Good luck to 'em, I say.'

Keene turned away, and as he did so he caught sight of a frigate anchored in mid-harbour and flying the French colours. He found a lighterman and had himself rowed out to her. As the boat drew close Keene read the ship's name on her stern – *L'Embuscade*.

There was only a skeleton crew aboard and the duty officer had little enthusiasm for helping a strange civilian. He was reclining in a chair on the quarterdeck reading a novel and scarcely looked up as the visitor was presented to him.

'I have a French citizen in urgent need of medical attention,' Keene urged.

The lieutenant shrugged. 'Dr Caillot's ashore. Devil knows where you'll find him.'

'Can't you give me some suggestion where to look? My friend is seriously ill.'

'Surely there are plenty of doctors in Charleston.'

'I'm sure my friend would rather be attended by one of his own countrymen. He's a very important man. His name is Genet. He's the representative of the Paris government.'

'Citizen Genet?' The officer dropped his book and jumped to his feet. 'Why didn't you say so? Where is he? No matter; tell me as we go. I'll help you find Caillot.'

He called for a boat and within minutes he and Keene were being rowed back to the quay. During the short journey the Englishman summarised the events of the afternoon. The lieutenant's opinion of Genet's hecklers was succinct. 'Royalist scum!'

'It's true, then, all the slaves in French colonies have been emancipated?'

'Not by Paris – not yet, but it's only a matter of time. It's a vital part of the new order, the new world. Captain Bowen is committed to tracking down every slave trader he can find.'

'Bowen? That doesn't sound like a French name.'

'The *Embuscade* has a mixed crew. Nationality is of little importance to us. We are a brotherhood, a revolutionary brotherhood.'

'Should you not be in European waters, fighting the British?'

'Captain Bowen believes we do better service here, showing our American brothers where their true interests lie.'

'And recruiting men and ships in American ports to the
revolutionary cause?'

The Frenchman looked suspiciously at the man sitting
opposite in the boat's stern. 'You ask many questions. Are
you sure you are a friend of Citizen Genet?'

'You'll see for yourself when we've found the doctor,'
Keene rejoined, standing as the boat nudged the seaweed-
stained harbour wall.

That task took them the best part of an hour but eventually
they ran Caillot to earth in a brothel in one of the streets
hugging the harbour. By the time they had torn him from
his pleasures and Keene had guided him to the warehouse,
Genet was much recovered. He was sitting on a chair, drinking copiously from a pocket flask and obviously enjoying
being fussed over by some of his supporters, who, having
evaded their pursuers, had gone in search of their champion.
Keene noted that Jensen was not among them. Someone had
sent for the diplomat's carriage and minutes later it arrived.
Keene stayed until Genet and the doctor had mounted the
conveyance and set off for the plenipotentiary's hotel. Then,
having nothing better to occupy him, he wandered back to
the harbour.

The skirmish which had so excited the denizens of the
waterfront was long over and everyone was going about
their business. Keene bought a jug of ale and a pie at a
seamen's tavern and sat by the open doorway looking out
across the anchorage. When a couple of lightermen came to
the same table he asked them if they knew anything about
the excitements of the afternoon.

'Disappointing.' One of the men rubbed a sleeve across
his froth-flecked beard. 'Just a spat between a couple of
frigates.'

'British and French?'

'Yeah,' said the second boatman, who had a livid scar
across one cheek. 'By all accounts the Frenchie had the

weather gauge but the king's ship got away and slipped into harbour. No stomach for a fight. Pity!'

'Why do you say that?' Keene asked.

Scarface took a swig of ale, belched loudly, then explained. 'There's good money paid for prizes to be turned into privateers and work for our boys manning them.'

'Who's paying for all this?'

'Why, the French government, of course, or leastwise their man over here – Monsure Jennet, or some such.'

Keene nodded slowly. Genet! Of course. That explained why he was so popular with the seamen and also why some of the wealthy mercantile community made common cause with the dispossessed plantation owners in wanting his blood.

'But surely all this is illegal,' he suggested.

His companions laughed throatily. 'Illegal? Course it's illegal. Take a look at that notice over there.'

Keene rose and scrutinised a scrap of printed paper pinned to the wall. It read:

REWARD
20 DOLLARS

will be paid for information leading to the conviction of anyone found guilty of dealing in vessels, ship's equipment or cargo the property of nations with which the United States of America are at peace.

The governor and legislature of the state of South Carolina condemn in the highest degree any citizens who may personally engage in acts of hostility at sea against any of the nations party to the present war and will take all measures to bring any such to punishment. The governor and legislature of the state of South Carolina condemn in the highest degree the practice of commissioning and manning vessels on behalf of any of the belligerent parties and will take all necessary measures to apprehend and bring to justice any found guilty of such acts.

'That seems pretty straightforward,' Keene commented, resuming his seat.

'Ain't no one claimed the reward yet,' Scarface said, 'leastwise no one among the harbour folk.'

Keene finished his meal and wandered out on to the quay. Dusk was turning the sea gunmetal grey and blurring the outlines of all the ships but he could distinguish the shape of a British frigate standing just inside the harbour mouth. Its still unfurled mainsail was holed, an obvious sign of recent conflict, but beyond that he could make out no other details. He was just turning to walk back towards the town when he felt a hand on his shoulder.

'George, by all that's wonderful! Is it really you?'

The voice was familiar, sickeningly familiar. Keene looked into the face of Captain Charles Hawkestone, the man who was married to the woman who had borne Keene's son, the woman who should have been his own wife.

Eight

Speechless, Keene could only stare, open-mouthed, at the boyish features of the man before him in the crisp blue and white of one of His Britannic Majesty's naval captains. He could scarcely recognise, let alone control, the emotions that skirmished within him. With this man he had shared the brotherhood of combat. Hawkestone had rescued him from the frenzy of Revolutionary France. The two friends had shared their profoundest thoughts and Keene could not find it in himself to hate the naive, good-natured soul that was Charles Hawkestone. Yet this was the man who, in simple-minded patriotism, had eagerly entered the service of the devious Sir Thomas Challoner and become his emissary upon the high seas. Above all, Hawkestone was the man who had stolen from him his beloved Thérèse.

He allowed his hand to be shaken and forced a smile to his lips. 'Charles, you're the last man . . . What brings you here? Is that . . . ?' He nodded towards the warship in the bay.'

The younger man laughed. 'Yes, that's the old *Promise*. We've had some stirring times aboard her, eh?'

'You're still working for Challoner, then?'

'Yes, George, as you are. I suppose that means we still have to keep secrets from each other.'

Keene noted the anxious frown that passed quickly over Hawkestone's face. He would later wish that he had taken more note of it. He said, 'I think Sir Thomas even keeps secrets from himself. Can you tell me where you're bound this trip?'

Hawkestone clapped an arm round Keene's shoulder. 'No mystery about that. We're for the Indies. Things are devilishly confused there and our master wants a first-hand account of what's going on. Still, we're in no hurry to sail. A few repairs to be done. We had a set-to with a damned Frenchie today. Could have blown her out of the water but you know what Sir Thomas thinks about "needless exposure to risk". We were obliged to turn tail. Deuced humiliating! Anyway, it's an ill wind that blows no man to profit, as the saying goes. And here we are together again, George. You must come aboard. I've a few bottles of something special I've been saving for an occasion and I can't think of a better excuse to open 'em.' He steered his companion towards a flight of stone steps that led down from the quay to where the *Promise*'s longboat was tethered.

Keene drew back. 'Good of you, Charles, but the celebration must wait. Things to attend to . . . Urgent.' He was finding words difficult. There were too many memories, too many emotions getting in the way. He grasped Hawkestone's hand and pressed it firmly. 'God go with you, Charles.' He turned abruptly.

He had gone only a few paces when Hawkestone called out, 'George, there's something I need to tell you – about Thérèse.'

The name stopped Keene in his tracks. He wheeled around. 'Thérèse? Something's wrong? By God, if you've . . .'

'She's in the best of health, but . . . Look, George, this is not the place . . . Come over to the *Promise*, where we can talk properly.'

Keene shook his head. He needed time to think and had no wish to revisit the frigate with its mixed memories. 'No, Charles, not the *Promise*. Give me an hour, then come and sup with me at my inn. It calls itself a hotel – the Union Hotel. Anyone can direct you.' He turned and almost fled along the quay.

The Union Hotel had pretensions to gentility. Among the

facilities it offered its exclusive clientele was the novelty of a small chamber provided with half a dozen tables where they could take meals in relative seclusion. The management prided themselves on providing an ambience where members of the American elite and visiting dignitaries could eat in a style that bore some resemblance to that which they enjoyed in their own homes. Glass, porcelain and silver adorned the tables and a corps of liveried attendants were on hand to see to the customers' every need. Keene had ensconced himself at a corner table by the time his punctual guest arrived.

Hawkestone entered attended by two seamen in crisp shore trim who stationed themselves by the door. He handed his bicorn to a flunky and seated himself opposite his host.

Keene eyed the gleaming white uniform lapels and the neatly tied stock. 'Captaincy suits you, Charles,' he observed.

The other man grinned. 'I'll own it's good to have more of the giving of orders than the taking of 'em.'

They made small talk, each now reticent about opening up to the other. Only when they had demolished a dish of chops, ordered a second bottle of claret and had a quartered capon placed between them did Keene venture, 'You had something to tell me about Thérèse?'

A waiter stepped forward to refill their glasses. Hawkestone took from him the dark bottle bearing the hotel's name on its shoulder and waved him away with the order, 'Bring us another.'

'She speaks of you often, George, and thinks of you more. That I know full well.'

'I'm sorry,' Keene said, but did not feel it. 'Your life together shouldn't be haunted by regrets about the past.'

Hawkestone dropped his fork and stared intently across the table. 'George, I never realised how much she felt . . . you felt . . . I'd never . . . Oh, dammit! Can't you see what I'm trying to say?' The young man's cheeks glowed with embarrassment and wine. 'I'm sorry. The moment I met Thérèse I was . . . '

'You felt the sharp prick of Cupid's dart,' Keene supplied, not without a tinge of bitterness.

'More like a regular broadside,' Hawkestone agreed wryly.

'No doubt she was also holed below the waterline.'

The other man shook his head emphatically. 'No, that's just the point. I believed that at first and, of course, I wanted to believe it. But it ain't so. Oh, she likes me well enough and I don't believe she would ever think of being unfaithful.'

'Then you're a fortunate man indeed, Charles. Few husbands could say as much – particularly husbands with beautiful young wives.'

'Look, you mustn't blame her for not telling me how deeply she felt about you. It was my fault. I behaved like a love-crazed boy. I was determined to possess her and she lacked the spirit to resist.'

'Well, that's hardly surprising after all she'd been through.' Keene thought of the terrified French girl who had seen her sister raped and her father imprisoned under the old regime, who had witnessed that same father turned into an avenging fanatic in the early days of the Revolution, who had tried, unsuccessfully, to escape from her ravaged and bleeding country only to be dragged back to Paris and there gain her life at the price of being married off to an aged Jacobin. He recalled painfully, as he did often, their brief love affair amidst the chaos of the French capital and his flight with a pregnant Thérèse to the coast where she had been entrusted to the care of Charles Hawkestone. 'You could provide her with security and comfort. She could become the future Lady Hawkestone, married to a man who would inherit a title and a large Wiltshire estate. You were no less than she deserved after years of suffering. What could I have ever offered her?'

Hawkestone sighed. 'She would have resisted my advances and waited for you if it hadn't been for little Georgie. She told me as much a few weeks ago. She wanted a settled life for the boy and she knew something of the dangerous work you were committed to.'

'Then, Charles, everything is for the best and you have nothing to reproach yourself for.'

The captain poured more wine. He scowled suddenly. 'Devil take you, George! Stop trying to make this harder for me than it already is. The fact is she's losing me as well as you. This war's getting worse by the week. First it was just France. Then it spread to most of Europe. Now it's infesting the colonies and probably America. You and I know the end of it ain't in sight yet. I'll be at sea for years, lucky to get home once in a while. Chances are that one day I won't get home at all. So, you see—'

Keene interrupted him. 'You owe it to them to make sure that doesn't happen.'

'By refusing to serve my country? No, George, that isn't an option. I can't lay up my sword till this war is over.' He paused, then added slowly, 'But you could take her right away from it.'

Keene stared open-mouthed at his companion.

Hawkestone continued: 'Don't you see, George, it's fate – meeting you like this. I've known for some time that I'd never be able to make Thérèse really happy; that she pined for you, was worried about you. Then you disappeared without trace. I wrote to Challoner asking if he knew where you were but, of course, he told me nothing. It was as though you'd died, and I thought Thérèse would gradually come to terms with never seeing you again.' He smiled broadly. 'But here you are. Everything can work out as it should.'

Keene looked across the table in bewilderment. 'Charles, I don't altogether understand what you're saying, but whatever it is it's madness. I am, as you say, dead to Thérèse. That's the way it must stay . . . '

'No, George. I'm not the brightest of men, I haven't had as much book-learning as you, but I've never seen anything more clearly than this. You come back to England in the

91

Promise and you see Thérèse and together we sort out some arrangement. You and she can be together and I can go back to sea knowing that Thérèse and Georgie are in the best possible—'

'Stop!' Keene held up a hand. 'This is the most ridiculous proposal I've ever heard. For a start, I've no intention of going back to England.' He leaned forward and lowered his voice. 'I wouldn't tell anyone else this and you must promise to treat it in confidence: I intend to put myself well beyond the reach of Sir Thomas Challoner, and to stay there. As for Thérèse – well, to be blunt, Charles, she is your responsibility. You are the one who has to make a choice. Do you want your family or a naval career? I'm afraid you can't use me as a way out of your dilemma.'

'Damme, George, you sound like a canting, puritanical Wesleyan!' Hawkestone glowered angrily. 'Do you deny that you still love Thérèse?'

'No, of course . . . but that's beside—'

'Then you have a chance to make her happy, and yourself, and me. You say the choice is mine but it isn't. It's yours. I beg you to make the right decision.'

Keene shook his head firmly. 'It's no good, Charles. I *have* made my decision. I go my own way and so must you and Thérèse. I pray we all find the rest and happiness we deserve.'

There was a long pause. Hawkestone sat back in his chair. At last he said, 'I'm sorry, George. This has all come as a shock to you. I never was any good at diplomacy. Just come straight out with what's on my mind. Give yourself some time – a few hours – to think over what I've said. I'll come back here in the morning before we sail. You can give me your final answer then.'

'You can come, and welcome, but I shall say the same then as I say now.'

Hawkestone beckoned to one of his men. 'Well, we'll see. Now let's talk of other things. I promised you some decent wine and here it is.'

The seaman placed a bottle on the table and Hawkestone drew the cork. 'This port has been in my father's cellar at Collingbourne for at least twenty years.' He filled the glasses and raised his as he proposed a toast. 'To the future – whatever it may hold.'

Keene nodded and drank deeply. Hawkestone was right; the wine was good. A little on the sweet side perhaps. Then he noticed that his companion was looking at him intently – and that he had not tasted his own wine. He opened his mouth to say something but the words would not form. He blinked several times to clear his vision, which seemed suddenly blurred. His head was unaccountably heavy. He tried to raise a hand to stop it falling forward but there was no strength in his limbs. He slumped across the table and everything went black.

TOUSSAINT

'O you Africans, my brothers . . . the blood of so many victims cries for vengeance, and human and divine justice cannot delay to confound the guilty.'

Toussaint l'Ouverture

Nine

K eene awoke to find himself in a confined space, and one that was rocking from side to side. His head throbbed. He was sweating and his mouth felt as though it was full of sand. He tried to force himself to emerge from what he thought must be a meaningless nightmare. Slowly, painfully slowly, his surroundings swam into clearer focus. He was in a cot suspended from the ceiling of a small room. The drapes were drawn back and light came into the tiny chamber beyond through a small window. When, at last, recognition struck him he knew he was dreaming. This was a place he had been before – a first lieutenant's berth on the frigate *Promise*. He turned to the wall and closed his eyes. But sleep had finished with him and minutes later he sat up to acknowledge the reality that he was in Hawkestone's ship and that that ship was under sail.

There was sea water in a metal jug on a stand by the bed. Keene dowsed his face and stared at its reflection in a small mirror fixed to the wall. Fair hair straggling almost to his shoulders framed cheeks that were sunken and sallow. A day's growth of beard shadowed his jaw. His eyes were listless beneath heavy lids. He took a couple of deep breaths, then felt in the pit of his stomach a surge of nausea that sent him rushing from the cabin and out to the quarter gallery.

He reached the rail just in time. When he had finished vomiting, he stared out across the water. The American coastline was a blur on the clouded horizon and the *Promise* was making good speed away from it under full sail. Keene stared down into the swirling eddies of grey-green water,

too weak to face Hawkestone's latest treachery or even his
own anger.

'Ah, there you are then, George.' The *Promise*'s young
captain came to lean over the rail at his side.

Keene did not look up. 'Here I am, but why?'

'George –' Hawkestone's tone was subdued – 'you've
every right to be furious with me. I don't feel very proud
of myself. But there were reasons and I promise I'll answer
all your questions. But you're not up to it at the moment.
What you need now is to fill your stomach. There's food
in my cabin. Come along.'

Keene did not move. 'I've had my fill of your hospitality.'

Hawkestone persisted. 'Please, George, there's things you
don't know and you must get your strength up before I
explain fully.'

'Whatever "explanation" you offered, how could I believe
you?' For the first time Keene turned to look at his abduc-
tor. He read uncertainty and embarrassment in the young
man's face.

'I deserve the rebuke but I promise you this: if, when
you've heard what I have to say you still want to return
to America, I'll take you back at the first opportunity.'

Keene allowed himself to be led to the great cabin where
cheese and bread and salt beef and ale had been laid out.
There Hawkestone left him to eat in solitude. About one
thing the captain was right: food was the answer to his
physical wretchedness. He took his time over the meal and
while he ate he did a great deal of thinking. By the time he
joined Hawkestone on the quarterdeck he had some pointed
questions to ask.

The captain was staring aloft to where topmen were
unfurling the main topgallant. 'Wind's fallen away steadily
since dawn,' he muttered as Keene reached the top of the
companionway. 'Calms can last days or weeks in these
latitudes. It could be a month before we reach Barbados.'

'Oh, so you *are* bound for the West Indies, then. That at least wasn't a lie.'

Hawkestone drew him to the larboard rail. 'George, almost every word I spoke last night was the truth; 'pon my honour it was.'

Keene sneered. '"Almost"? I've read somewhere that half the truth is the greater lie.'

Hawkestone leaned against the rail and stared out across the listless ocean. The sun was halfway to its zenith and shifting pools of light lay like oil on the sea's turgid surface. 'It was never my intention to keep anything from you,' he said. 'But back there in Charleston you simply wouldn't have listened. When you refused my invitation to come aboard I had to resort to . . . George, I'm sorry, but I had to make you hear what I have to say.'

'Well, congratulations on achieving your objective,' Keene responded cynically. 'Since I don't intend to jump overboard, you have a captive audience. But let me make matters a little easier for you. My abduction has the stench of a typically malodorous Challoner plot. Am I right?'

The captain nodded.

'Of course. I should have spotted it straight away. The odds against you bumping into me by chance in Charleston were prodigious. The only way you could know where to look for me was by discovering my itinerary.'

'You're absolutely right. The *Promise* brought Sir Thomas from England and he introduced me to Hamilton, who later passed on information from your reports, so that I'd know where to look. However,' Hawkestone gave a nervous laugh, 'it was certainly a shock finding you so soon. I'd rehearsed my lines a hundred times but I very nearly bungled them.'

'It would certainly have been a pity to mangle the script written by so accomplished a playwright as Sir Thomas. All that melodrama about poor Thérèse pining for me.' Keene laughed. 'You were very good and I was vain enough to believe it.'

Hawkestone turned abruptly to face him. 'No, there

you're wrong. Every word of that was true and came from the heart.'

'You seriously expect me to believe that the little grey fox didn't put you up to it?'

Hawkestone's forehead wrinkled in a frown of concentration. 'Look, George, this was the way of it. Challoner knows you're his best man and he's desperate to have you back in England. He realises the only bait he can use is Thérèse. So he ordered me to find you and spin you a yarn about reuniting you with her. His orders were that I was to bring you back by hook or by crook. He even gave me the drug to put in the wine as a last resort. He thinks of everything. Curious thing is that Challoner's "story" actually makes sense. The more I brooded on it the more I realised that I'd been thinking much the same thing myself – well, not "thinking" exactly but sensing, you know, deep inside.' He looked awkwardly down at his buckled shoes. 'You do believe me, don't you, George?'

Keene thought for a moment, then said, 'If all you say is true then you're disobeying Challoner's orders by telling me.'

Hawkestone nodded. 'I made up my mind that when I found you I'd make a clean breast of everything. Leave you to make your own decision.'

'Sir Thomas won't be very pleased when you return without me.'

'George, you have my solemn promise that if you refuse to return to England I'll do nothing more to persuade or force you. As for Challoner, devil take him! I'm tired of his service. I didn't join the navy to go skulking round the seven seas avoiding engagement with the enemy. The *Promise* is a fighting ship and it's time she started fighting. The crew is getting devilish restive. They want action. They want prize money. They want to be able to go home and boast of the Frenchies they captured or blew out of the water.'

Keene considered the younger man's response for several moments. At last he said, 'I still don't see what you had in

100

mind for Thérèse. If you took me back Challoner would soon have me doing his bidding in France or somewhere equally unpleasant and dangerous. I'd be just as likely as you to end up a casualty of war. Truth is, it's no thanks to Sir Thomas that I'm still alive at all.'

Hawkestone's eyes lit up. He spoke with a new eagerness. 'But I've thought it all out. As soon as we've finished in the Antilles, we make best speed for England. We put into Weymouth and ride over to Collingbourne. We collect Thérèse and Georgie and enough money to give you a decent new start in life. Then I pack you all into a carriage, and within hours you'll be on the road to Southampton where you can take the next passenger ship to America, or wherever else takes your fancy. Then I resume my voyage to London and report that I was able to find no trace of George Keene in that vast continent on the other side of the Atlantic.' He laughed. 'You see, George, it's simple – like all good plans.'

Keene shook his head sharply. 'So simple that Challoner would see through it like a pane of glass. He'd have you clapped in irons and court-martialled before you knew what was happening.'

'Not if . . . '

'Charles, don't ever make the mistake of underestimating that man. Beneath that urbane exterior there's a fanatic. That's why he's so good at what he does. It needs someone unprincipled and determined to counter the devils who've taken over France. In a way I admire him. But I fear him more, because if his brand of ruthlessness and cynical manipulation represents the only alternative to Revolution and anarchy, then Heaven help us all. Whatever you do, Charles, promise me that you will never try to pit your wits against Thomas Challoner.'

'Oh, come, George . . . '

'No, Charles!' Keene thumped the rail with his fist. 'Listen to me. Our master is desperate to have me back. You've seen the lengths he's gone to to achieve that end. I was foolish enough to suppose that a few thousand miles of Atlantic Ocean would deter him. Now we both know how wrong I was. If he even suspected that you had deliberately thwarted him he'd not hesitate to make an example of you "*pour encourager les autres*". His vengeance could even extend to Thérèse. He's always resented my forcing his hand over her rescue.'

Hawkestone was crestfallen. He began to pace the quarter-deck slowly. By the mizzenmast he stopped and turned abruptly. 'But in that case . . . '

'Yes.' Keene nodded gravely. 'In that case we already have a problem. Here I am aboard the *Promise*. All your men have seen me. If I were to disappear somewhere between here and London Challoner would ask questions. He would pay for information. How many of these fellows –' he waved a hand towards the main deck – 'do you think would resist such a temptation?'

Hawkestone raised his hands to his head. 'My God, George, I didn't think . . . What have I done?'

Keene smiled ruefully. 'No less than one of his Majesty's loyal officers should have done – your duty. You have obeyed orders. You were sent to apprehend George Keene and, by a brilliant ruse, you have succeeded. That is precisely how things stand at the moment.'

'But what . . . '

'What are we going to do? I've no idea, Charles, but don't look so glum. We have the rest of the voyage to work out something.' He looked aloft to the flapping sails. 'And if you don't get the wind you want it could be a long one.'

The weather improved. In fact, at one stage the *Promise* caught the outer edge of a hurricane and was, for a couple of days, thrown across the ocean at a speed which strained every sheet and timber. She put in at Nassau in the Bahamas where Hawkestone and Keene climbed the hill to Government House to pay their respects to the governor. They were received by his wife, who explained that her husband had gone to London to demand aid in the crisis that was threatening the islands. She received them in the shade of a poinciana grove overlooking a sloping lawn fringed by brilliant bougainvillaeas and served them rum punch chilled with ice from the governor's own ice house.

She eagerly quizzed Hawkestone for news of the Admiralty's plans and was clearly disappointed that he could tell her little. 'The fleet here is in desperate need of augmentation,' she explained. 'Without adequate protection the entire civilisation we have built up here will vanish. The islands will revert to barbarism, the plantations will fall into decay, the owners will be ruined – those who are fortunate enough to escape with their lives – and the British economy will collapse. We have built a new garrison at Fort Fincastle but without the soldiers to man it . . . Yellow fever takes such a toll of our military . . . I've had to send my daughters back to England . . . Captain, the Admiralty has no comprehension . . . '

Hawkestone interrupted the breathless catalogue of disaster by quietly suggesting that the war with France was stretching the navy's resources.

'Poh, France!' She responded with a fervour that, Keene thought, came strangely from this genteel lady who sat before them, clad in pale blue silk, her soft features artistically rouged. 'All those ministers in London can think of is their stupid European war! What is about to burst upon us here is a revolt of the savages. French, English – what does it matter when Christian civilisation is at stake? Nassau and Grand Bahama are already bursting with refugees from the French colonies. And why? Because their government in Paris was too short-sighted to provide the ships and men necessary to preserve order. They were warned – five years ago and often since – but they did nothing. And now they have lost Saint Domingue to the pestilential blacks and their other territories will follow – *and* ours!'

Keene radiated sympathy. 'The rumour in America is that

Paris will soon give in and announce the emancipation of the slaves.'

The lady glared. 'Not Paris – even the Jacobins would not be so mad. No, it was that little coward, Leger-Felicité Sonthonax, the governor of Saint Domingue. Instead of standing up to this Toussaint creature and defending his people to the last man he surrendered his sword. Think of it! A white general going on bended knee to a mere black slave!'

'Toussaint? Who is this Toussaint?' Hawkestone asked.

'A typical brigand.' She waved a hand dismissively. 'He's gathered a rabble round him and leads them in looting and pillaging the homes of his betters. You'll hear many stories about him in the islands, stories that grow and grow in the telling. If you take my advice you'll give no heed to any of them. If anyone tries to tell you that this Toussaint is a "hero", a "messiah", remember that he's just an ignorant black.'

Keene thought but did not say that a man who could overwhelm a French garrison and its general and spread fear over thousands of miles of island settlements must be more than a brigand.

Information that Hawkestone and members of his crew picked up at other ports of call confirmed some of what the governor's wife had told them. The name 'Toussaint' was whispered everywhere. Or more frequently 'L'Ouverture', 'Gap-tooth', for, like condotierri and pirates of old, he used a physical attribute to ensure instant recognition and strike fear into his enemies. He was the scourge of the colonial oppressors, the saviour who was going to free the tens of thousands of slaves who worked the plantations all over the Caribbean. However, there was considerable confusion about the success of the black revolt, and European officials were not disposed to share the panic that had sent the Governor of the Bahamas scurrying back to England with his daughters. For them the possibility of an inferior race gaining the upper hand was unthinkable. If they acknowledged at all that Toussaint had achieved an advantage, they only conceded that it was temporary. He was, after all, a mere opportunist taking advantage of the conflict between the great powers to gain an evanescent 'freedom' that he, in common with all black 'children', was simply not equipped to handle. Keene listened to the petty caesars, enclosed in their brittle globes of local authority, repeat the same affirmations and prejudices in settlement after settlement. He heard them all reiterate to Captain Hawkestone the need for those reinforcements from Britain and her allies which could not fail to redress the status quo ante and put the ungrateful blacks firmly back in their place.

In the second week of December the *Promise* anchored in the port of Kingston, Jamaica, the closest British colony to Saint Domingue. As Keene and Hawkestone sat in the great cabin on the evening of their arrival, the captain produced from a locked chest a bulky sealed envelope on which was written in a neat hand Keene instantly recognised, 'To be opened immediately prior to reaching the coastal waters of Saint Domingue'. Hawkestone pushed to one side the remains of their meal and laid the packet on the table between them.

'Our master's latest instructions,' Keene observed.

Hawkestone nodded and tapped the envelope with a long forefinger. 'Before we open it perhaps it would be a good idea to go over what we know for fact about the situation here.'

'Agreed, though it's deuced difficult to disentangle fact from rumour. Just how pivotal is this black hero in the future of the colonies?'

'Everyone seems to agree that he started his revolt before the Revolution began.'

'And when it did begin he took all his followers across the border into Spanish Santo Domingo to help them overthrow his old masters.'

'Hah!' Hawkestone snorted. 'Sounds like a typical mercenary, selling his sword to the highest bidder.'

Keene sounded doubtful. 'Or a genuine visionary whose only loyalty is to his own people.'

'But when Governor Sonthonax declared freedom for the slaves Toussaint still did not make his peace. He saw he was on the winning side. French settlers were fleeing in droves, leaving their homes, their land and their possessions for him and his mob to grab.'

'Or he may have had the foresight to realise that Sonthonax was only yielding to *force majeure* and would reimpose servitude as soon as he had got control back into his own hands.'

Hawkestone looked puzzled. 'George, the man is a savage. His father or grandfather was dragged out of the trees in the African jungle. You can't think him capable of sophisticated political judgement.'

Keene shrugged. 'Well, let's see what Sir Thomas has to say.'

Hawkestone broke the seal and spread two sheets of heavy paper on the table. He began to read.

Captain Hawkestone, by now you should have Mr Keene with you and it will be advantageous for you to make him party to these instructions. What is required is any intelligence that may have a bearing on our conflict with France and the formation of our military strategy. You should understand that Mr Pitt's counsels are divided between those who see the West Indies as the key to victory over the current regime in Paris and those who believe that all our energies should be husbanded for the European struggle. Trade with Saint Domingue is the cornerstone of France's economy. Rendering assistance to our Spanish allies in the neighbouring colony would destabilise that economy and certainly damage her ability to expand her military activities across her borders. However, the counter-argument proposed is that a war of attrition would, of necessity, be protracted and costly. There are those who urge a yet more 'forward' policy. I quote from a recent communiqué received from Barbados: 'Saint Domingue is of vast, vast importance to Britain. Our West Indian possessions are comparatively deficient, diminutive, widely extended and, therefore, little capable of defence. It should be our objective to extend our sway over the whole island of Hispaniola, currently divided between Santo Domingo and Saint Domingue. As well as providing safe havens for a fleet which would ensure our command of the area, this would give Britain a monopoly of all trade in sugar, indigo, cotton and coffee. It would provide such a boost to home industry as would dissuade future migration of artisans to America.' Against this it is urged that the enormous expenditure in men and materiél necessary to extend and sustain our colonial interests would seriously weaken our position in Europe. The navy's intelligence system may be relied upon to provide information as to the current disposition of the enemy's defences but their lordships of the Admiralty will put their own gloss on any intelligence they make available to the government. What is required is a *cool* political appraisal of the overall situation. How are the various French authorities disposed to the new Jacobin regime in Paris? How stable are the various colonial societies? Who are the leaders in the French settlements? Would they be disposed to place themselves under the protection of His Britannic Majesty? You are to glean all you can pertinent to these questions in as short a space of time as possible and then to proceed to Barbados. A military expedition under the joint leadership of Vice Admiral Jervis and Lieutenant-General Grey should arrive there before

the end of the year. You are to wait for them and you are at liberty to furnish them with such information OF A PURELY MILITARY NATURE as may be of assistance to them. You are then to proceed back to London with all despatch, together with Mr Keene.
Thomas Challoner

Hawkestone sat back. 'No mention of this Toussaint fellow.'

With a shrug Keene said, 'Challoner probably hadn't heard of him when he wrote and if he had he would have paid little attention. Here Toussaint's bloody insurrection is wreaking havoc, depriving thousands of settlers of their livelihood and costing many lives. In London a distant slave revolt must seem very small beer.'

'You see the last words of my orders: "together with Mr Keene". Have you worked out a way of escaping Challoner's clutches?'

'Not in detail,' Keene replied thoughtfully, 'But clearly it will be necessary for me to die.'

'George!' Hawkestone looked shocked.

His friend laughed. 'Don't worry, Charles. I don't mean that literally. We just have to convince Sir Thomas that I really am dead. And he will take some convincing.'

'Why do you say that?'

'Because,' Keene said grimly, 'the little grey fox once fabricated my death to serve his own purposes. If he were now to hear that I had had a fatal accident his first thought would be that I was trying to beat him at his own game. He would not rest until he had made absolutely sure that my demise was genuine.'

'So, what do you propose?'

'I have some ideas but I can't share them for the moment. However, I can tell you that it will have to be something spectacular with plenty of witnesses.'

At that moment there was a tap at the door. It was opened by Hawkestone's cabin boy, who stood in the entrance and announced, 'Major General Williamson, Captain. Er, Governor Williamson,' he added nervously.

The man who bustled in was in his late fifties, white-haired, bronzed and wearing the Gabrielet tunic with blue and gold facings of an infantry officer. 'Well, well, well, Charlie Hawkestone,' the visitor boomed, advancing with hand outstretched. 'You're the very image of your father. Last time I saw you, you were so high.' He tapped the top of the table.

Hawkestone looked puzzled. 'Sir, I . . . '

'Don't remember me?' Williamson asked affably. 'Well, why should you? It's years since I had the pleasure of Collingbourne hospitality. The army's kept me abroad most of those years.'

Hawkestone offered a chair and a glass of claret, both of which were gratefully accepted. He introduced Keene to the newcomer. 'You're doubly welcome, sir,' he said, 'as a friend of my father and as his Majesty's representative in Jamaica.'

'How is Sir William?' the older man asked, draining his glass at a gulp and holding it out for a refill. Without waiting for a reply, he went on. 'I met him first in '58. He was captain of the troopship *Scipio*, which conveyed part of my regiment out to Canada. Then, as luck would have it, he commanded the convoy that took me to Boston in '75. Just in time for the fiasco of Bunker Hill,' he added sourly. 'Damned rebellious ingrates! We drove the French out for 'em, helped 'em to defend themselves against the Indians and what do we get in return? Booted out!' He hammered his empty glass down on the table and watched as Hawkestone poured claret from a fresh bottle. 'Still, it looks as though we shall have the last laugh.'

'In what way, sir?' Keene asked.

The old soldier leaned forward, his eyes alight with patriotic zeal. 'The French Caribbean empire is falling apart. There is nothing to stop us adding their possessions to our own – as long as Pitt and his friends play their cards right. Once the Indies are ours we control all colonial trade. Then we shall soon hear the American rebels sing a new song. They'll be excluded from trade with the Indies and they'll have to pay our prices for cotton, sugar, rum and coffee, as well as all our own manufactured goods.'

'But aren't they developing their own plantation economy?' Keene asked quietly.

'*And* we'll starve 'em of slaves,' the general continued as though he had not heard the interruption.

'Talking of slaves,' Hawkestone said, 'what do you know of this fellow Toussaint?'

'Deuced clever fellow.' Williamson sat back, took out a silver snuff box, sniffed up a generous pinch of the powder and offered it to his companions.

'The impression we've been given is that the man is an ignorant brigand,' Keene observed.

'And I'll wager you were told that by men who've never faced him in combat.' The soldier shook his head. 'First rule of good generalship: never underestimate your enemy. That was the mistake we made with Washington. Well, I've seen this blackamoor in action and I respect him. That don't mean to say I consider him a match for any seasoned British commander. I don't. And as for what passes as his "army" – well, they're a harlequin bunch and no mistake: blacks who don't know one end of a musket from the other; renegade half-castes who used to run the plantations and now have the ordering of men in battle; and a few monarchist soldiers and officers who hate being commanded by a slave but hate the French Revolutionaries even more.'

'They should be easy to overcome with well-armed British troops,' Hawkestone suggested.

'Well, young man, you'll be able to see the problem for yourself in a few days when you've landed me and my men.'

The captain raised his eyebrows in surprise. 'Sir, I have no authority . . . '

'You've my authority,' the general snapped as he reached

110

his hand for the bottle. 'Listen while I explain the situation to you. This black caesar took up arms against the local agents of the French Revolutionary regime, claiming to be a loyal servant of the Bourbons and styling himself "General of the Armies of the King for the Public Good".'

The more Keene heard about this extraordinary phenomenon the more intrigued he became. Now he asked, 'Is the man a genuine monarchist or just an opportunist taking advantage of the political chaos in France and her overseas possessions?'

The old soldier's thick eyebrows met in a frown and Keene guessed he was not accustomed to being interrupted in mid-anecdote. 'I wouldn't know what goes on in the beggar's mind,' Williamson said, 'and nor did the Spanish authorities in Santo Domingo. When Toussaint took a little band of followers over the border they welcomed him with open arms. They were stupid enough to think that they could use him. They'd let him lead cross-frontier raids to distract the Frogs while they got on with the serious business of invasion. They soon discovered that the black had other ideas. He was set on using them. From the safe haven of their territory he made forays into Saint Domingue, burning settlements, freeing slaves and building up a personal army that soon numbered more than five thousand. Soon it was this "mere savage" who was doing the invading, and the Dagos could no more control him than the Frogs could. He captured town after town in the north—' Williamson broke off suddenly. 'I need a map. Do you have anything suitable?'

Hawkestone opened one of the drawers in the chart chest beneath the table, pulled out several large sheets and spread them before him.

'This one'll do,' the general muttered, extracting a chart of the reefs and channels around Cuba, Saint Domingue and Jamaica that showed the island of Hispaniola like a large lobster with its claw open to the west. 'In the first six months of this year Toussaint overran most of the northern province of the colony, starting with Cap François, here on the coast, then up into the hill country to take Dondon, Marmelade, Plaisance and all the plantations in between. By August he was moving southwards towards the capital, Port au Prince. By that time the war had become a crusade to liberate all the slaves, which would, of course, mean destroying the economy completely.'

'General.' Keene risked another interjection. 'Didn't Governor Sonthonax issue an emancipation decree and didn't that give Toussaint all he had been fighting for?'

Williamson ran a finger round his neckband. 'Deuced hot in here! That's a good point you make, Keene, but you don't know what power does to men. Toussaint's a clever devil. He's an independent force, a force to be reckoned with and he ain't going to surrender his freedom of action. He knows well enough that everyone's out to manipulate him – the Spaniards, the governor, the plantation owners. As long as he has a growing army at his back why should he let himself be bribed or gulled into sharing his power with anyone? No, he continues his southward march and Sonthonax has been forced to fall back on Port au Prince. That's why we have to act now. We'll never get a better opportunity.'

'How did you gather all this detailed information?' Keene wanted to know.

'First rule of good generalship,' Williamson replied brusquely. 'First-rate intelligence. Knowing what the enemy's up to is worth an extra battalion. I have my agents over in Saint Domingue and anyway every ship that docks here brings fresh information. And pleas for help.'

'From fleeing plantation owners,' Keene suggested.

'Of course, lad. They don't give a groat for what government rules in Paris as long as their way of life isn't threatened. Day after day I was plagued with requests to take Saint Domingue under British protection. Week after week I sent to London for permission to invade. All the time this black was getting stronger and stronger and I was sitting here losing the military initiative. A couple of months ago I decided I couldn't wait any longer. First rule of good generalship: gain the initiative. I gathered together every man I could find and landed here in the south,' he prodded the map with a stubby forefinger, 'at Jeremie, with a force of nine hundred.'

'Not many,' Keene ventured.

'No, but enough.' For the next half-hour the general described in great detail the campaign he had led in recent weeks. The British had rapidly made themselves masters of all the southern coast but had lacked the manpower to sustain a siege of Port au Prince. 'That's why I had to come back,' he concluded. 'Raise reinforcements for a final push on the capital. I've a hundred and fifty fresh troops waiting on shore. I'll embark 'em in the morning and we can sail on the next tide.'

Two hours and three bottles later the general staggered across the deck and was helped into a boat. Hawkestone had tried to persuade him that the *Promise* was not equipped or provisioned to take on such a large extra complement. He insisted that his orders were to make the best speed to Barbados. He made no impression on Williamson's determination. The first rule of good generalship, he ruefully remarked to Keene, must be to bludgeon a way through all opposition.

Ten

With the dawn came the troops. When Keene emerged
onto the deck as the first rays of sunlight gilded the
treetops on the hills above the town, he saw Williamson's
infantry drawn up in ranks on the road before the waterfront
warehouses and shops. Within minutes the old soldier's boat
was alongside and he scrambled energetically aboard with
no indication of any after-effects of the previous night's
alcohol. He had obviously already given embarkation orders
because the first of his men arrived almost immediately.

The *Promise*'s crew were set to scurrying around finding
sleeping spaces for their guests where they would not
be too much in the way. This near-impossible task was
not accomplished without much cursing and shouting but
accomplished it eventually was and around mid-morning
Hawkestone's men, shouldering redcoats out of the way
and tripping over knapsacks, managed to weigh the anchor,
hoist sails and get the frigate under way. The next two
days, though uncomfortable, passed without incident, and
Williamson's men were duly landed at Petit Goeve, some
thirty miles from Port au Prince, where the bulk of the British
force was encamped.

Keene went ashore with the general, eager to see for
himself the little army which, according to Williamson,
was poised to capture the world's richest colony. Further
acquaintance with the fiery governor had left him in no
doubt that he was driven as much by personal ambition as by
fervent patriotism in his desire to conquer Saint Domingue.
There was something of the buccaneer about this old soldier

114

who carried the scars of many a battle and repeated, ad nauseam, tales of derring-do and high heroics. The days were long past when Jamaica had been the base for pirate bands who were the scourge of the Main, but their names and exploits were ingrained in the island's folklore and Williamson had about him something of the fabled Captain Morgan, who had crowned a colourful life ruling Jamaica as a personal fiefdom, only theoretically under the crown. Major General Adam Williamson was not the sort of royal representative content to wait upon orders from London, and Keene sensed that he was delighted to have received no clear answer to his requests for instructions (if, indeed, he had ever seriously sought them). It allowed him the freedom to mount his own crusade against republican France, conquer single-handedly that nation's most prized overseas possession, hugely increase Britain's commercial power, and fatally cripple her enemy. For such an accomplishment there could not fail to be generous recognition from the government – a sizeable pension, a peerage, an impressive country estate and that place in public life reserved for returned heroes.

Williamson had been equally assiduous in trying to gauge Keene's standing and importance. He was curious about why a civilian should be present aboard the *Promise* and, since Keene and Hawkestone returned only equivocal answers to his many questions, he concluded that the tall, quiet, well-travelled Englishman must be the representative of some person of great importance in court or government; perhaps even of the king himself. So, at least, Keene assumed from the increasing deference the older man showed him.

Now, as they rode the few miles to the British camp, Williamson outlined his strategy with the obvious intention not only of impressing Keene, but also of enlisting his aid.

'Port au Prince's landward defences are strong,' he explained. 'A simple siege could take months.'

'And, I imagine, a larger force than you have,' Keene suggested.

The general took out his snuff box and self-administered

Derek Wilson

a generous dose before commenting, 'That's as it may be but I'll allow an unimaginative, straightforward attack would be deuced hard. That leaves the only other option: a surprise assault – hit the enemy where he least expects it, like Wolfe at Quebec.'

Keene nodded sagely and said mischievously, 'Yes, surprise; the first rule of good generalship.'

'Precisely, Keene, precisely!' Williamson gave no sign of recognising the barb. 'Have I mentioned that I was with him?'

'With who?' Keene asked innocently.

Williamson scowled and kept his temper with difficulty. 'General Wolfe, Keene, General Wolfe. I was a mere lieutenant but I recognised his brilliance, as none of the senior officers did. They thought he was mad to land five thousand men in a narrow cove, the Anse de Foulon, right under a sheer escarpment that must take them an hour to scramble up. And the Frogs, well, they thought he wouldn't be mad enough to attempt it. Well, we all know the result. Surprise, you see, Keene. That's what won Quebec and that's what'll win us Port au Prince.'

They topped a rise and paused to look down on the narrow plain beyond. In the midst of it, a couple of miles away, stood the British encampment, a circular timber palisade within which were lined up rank upon rank of tents. Williamson turned to his impeccably dressed escort and ordered one of his lieutenants to ride on and have the company paraded for his inspection.

'So, what is your surprise plan, General?' Keene asked as they began the gradual descent.

'Sonthonax believes he's impregnable from the sea. Port au Prince is an excellent harbour. The island of Gonave stands in the middle of the bay and leaves only narrow channels either side for the approach of ships. There's very little room for a naval force to manoeuvre, so the Frogs have little need for heavy artillery defence on the seaward side. But what a fleet of ships can't do, one well-armed frigate

116

can. If the *Promise* slips up to the port entrance under cover of darkness and begins a battery the Frenchies'll panic, and in the confusion half my men will work along the coast by boat and storm the harbour defence at its weakest point. They'll fight their way to the south gate and open it.'

Keene studied the triumphant smile on the soldier's face. How simple military plans seemed when expressed in words. This proposal for the overthrow of the capital of Saint Domingue was a variant of Wolfe's daring and desperate ascent of the Heights of Abraham and Keene wondered how much of Williamson's strategy was a pastiche of techniques and manoeuvres learned from abler commanders. 'Have you discussed this with Hawkestone?' he asked.

'No, not yet.' The general fell silent for a few moments then asked, 'Have you known him long?'

'Less than a year.'

'Yet he thinks highly of you.'

'I hope so.'

'He's young – very young for such a command.'

'He's a very effective captain.'

'To be sure. To be sure. Yet he lacks that soundness of judgement that only experience can give. Now, you, Keene, you've seen a lot more of the world. I'll wager you've an instinct for recognising a bold but intelligent plan.'

'General, are you asking me to propose your scheme to the captain?'

Williamson shook his head resolutely. 'Propose? No. Just give me your support. Young Hawkestone is fidgeting to be away. Together we can make him see that his duty is to stay here till Port au Prince is taken.'

'And risk his ship being blown out of the water by the coastal battery?' Keene had a momentary vision of Challoner receiving the news that his spy vessel had been destroyed by deliberately sailing close in to the guns of a French fort.

'No real chance of that,' the general muttered. 'And

think of the prize: the whole colony in our hands. The Admiralty will reward him handsomely for his part in such an achievement.'

Keene searched for some way to deflect the zealot from his glorious obsession. 'Hawkestone's orders come from higher up than the Admiralty,' he said quietly.

'Who?'

Keene held a finger to his lips and shook his head. 'He has very precise instructions. If he was deflected from carrying them out there would be considerable discontent expressed – at the topmost level.'

Williamson scowled. 'Damned politicians!' Then he looked quickly at Keene and added the grudging concession, 'I suppose they know what they're doing.'

'Sir!' One of the general's officers moved alongside him, holding out a telescope. 'You might like to look at the camp.'

Williamson reined in his mount and set the glass to his eye. He groaned and seemed to sink in the saddle.

'Something wrong, General?' Keene enquired.

Without a word Williamson handed over the telescope. Keene focused on the palisade. It seemed to be intact and there were sentries manning their posts beside the gateway, which stood open. Everything appeared to be in order. Then he looked more closely at the small column emerging from the stockade. Three carts loaded with cloth-wrapped bundles, and accompanied by two files of soldiers moving with slow, measured tread. Theirs was a short journey. A few yards ahead lay a row of freshly dug graves. Beside them were many other mounds surmounted by rough wooden crosses.

The general's party reached the camp in silence. Keene had been among soldiers before but never had he encountered the atmosphere that greeted him now. There was none of the bustle and noise usually found in the lines. No men sharing ribald jokes. No non-commissioned officers shouting staccato orders. No trumpet calls. No drums. Only the subdued sounds of men sombrely getting on with jobs that had to be done.

Keene made his own way among the troops, stopping occasionally to talk to individuals or small groups. It took no time to discover the tragic truth. Of the eight hundred fit men the general had left here three weeks before, a third had succumbed to fever and a further fifty lay in a screened-off section of the camp, dying. Within the hour Keene returned to the *Promise*.

'What will the general do now?' Hawkestone asked, as they sat beneath an awning that had been rigged to shield the quarterdeck from the afternoon sun.

'When I left,' Keene said, 'he was ordering all the healthy men to move the camp to a new location a few miles away.'

'A sensible precaution.'

'Yes, but it's difficult to see what he can do with a depleted force of dispirited men.'

'Perhaps Admiral Jervis will come to his aid when his fleet arrives. We can do nothing more than go on to Barbados and report Williamson's plight.'

'Can we not? I was thinking as I rode back that Sonthonax is sure to know of this disaster. He would be foolish not to take advantage of it.'

'We have no way of knowing what his plans are.'

'Perhaps we could find out.'

Hawkestone looked up sharply at his friend. 'What in Heaven's name do you mean by that?'

'Your orders are to gather intelligence that may be useful to Jervis and to Challoner. What better than an accurate report of the strength and morale of the republican defenders of this colony?'

'Are you suggesting that we go into Port au Prince?'

'Certainly not.'

Hawkestone sighed with relief. 'I'm delighted to hear it.'

'You're command of the French language ain't up to it, Charles. I shall have to go alone.'

'That's absurd.'

'Why? The Frogs don't know me from Adam and I'm excellently practised at passing myself off as a Frenchman.'

'No, George! It's far too dangerous. I can't allow . . . '

Keene grinned. 'You can't stop me, Captain Hawkestone. I ain't under your command. And just think, in a few days I'll either be back safe and sound with valuable information to pass on to our fiery little general or I shall be a prisoner of Sonthonax. In that case you'll be able to report to Sir Thomas, with a clear conscience, that I was captured by the French and that it must be presumed that I have been executed as a spy.'

'And that'll probably be the truth.'

Keene laughed. 'Don't write my obituary until you have to, Charles. I've been in worse situations.'

Hawkestone brooded in silence for a while, sipping a beaker of rum, lemon juice and water, a concoction recommended by the Admiralty for men serving in tropical waters. Keene watched him thinking his methodical way through the problem. At last he set his beaker down on the deck and, with a smile of triumph on his face, he said, 'George, you're right. I can't give you orders, but I can give them to my own crew. I shall detail Lieutenant Cutt to accompany you.'

Keene shook his head vehemently. 'No, Charles, I work best alone and Cutt—'

'Sam Cutt speaks very good French. He comes from a family of diplomats. He ain't the brightest of individuals, which is probably why his father pushed him into the navy, but he's resourceful and strong. You'll find him an asset and, with him beside you, you'll stand some chance of getting out of Port au Prince alive.' Hawkestone stared defiantly at his companion. 'And there's one more thing you ought to know.'

'What's that.'

'If you refuse to take Cutt with you I'll have you clapped in the brig.'

Keene realised that argument was futile and for the sake

of his friend's peace of mind he gave in with a good grace, calculating as he did so that, if his chaperone got in the way, it should not be too difficult to give him the slip. Cutt was summoned and agreed to the plan with enthusiasm, happy, Keene assumed, to escape the routine of shipboard life and enjoy a spell ashore, even if that meant mingling with the enemy. He was a tall, thin sandy-haired man who, at thirty-three, already had a long naval career behind him. 'Razor' Cutt, as he was sardonically known among the crew, had a plodding brain and it had taken him three attempts to pass his lieutenant's exam. He was respected on the lower decks as an officer who went strictly by the book, and who, though largely humourless, was firm and even-handed in all his dealings.

Keene spent the rest of the day patiently tutoring his fellow conspirator in the art of adopting and sustaining a false identity. Sam Cutt was to become Sebastian Coutine and Keene adopted the identity of Georges Chêne, names sufficiently near their own in sound for the lieutenant to remember. They would pose as dispossessed plantation owners from a remote part of the north who had been forced to flee from their own rebellious slaves with little more than the clothes they stood up in. 'Do we have wives and children?' Cutt asked, entering enthusiastically into his role. Keene gently suggested that bachelordom would be more appropriate; they should keep their story as simple as possible for fear of entangling themselves in the coils of their own deception. Cutt frowned seriously and said he saw the point of that and Keene, aided by Hawkestone, continued the laborious process of drilling their pupil. Cutt's one redeeming feature was that he was bilingual and Keene urged him, repeatedly and insistently, to say as little as possible when they reached the town but to keep his ears open and register every scrap of information that might be useful. When, at last, Keene retired wearily to his cabin for the night it was with a serious sense of misgiving about the deal he had struck with Hawkestone.

Shortly before dawn he and his companion were rowed across to a point on the coast to the north of the harbour. From there they began their journey on foot towards the town. They wore the open-necked shirts and wide-brimmed straw hats which were common to white residents throughout the Caribbean and which they had bought in one of their ports of call. Both men were well bronzed after weeks under the tropical sun and certainly looked the part they were playing.

The suburbs of Port au Prince were still quiet as they walked through them towards the walls of the town. 'We'll wait until the traffic builds up,' Keene said in French. 'We should attract less attention going through the gate if we're part of a crowd.' They sat at a table in an open-air café and listened to the conversations of passers-by. Women complained to each other about the prices of bread and vegetables. Their husbands discussed the worsening situation in the North and the iniquity of ships' captains who were offering passage to Europe or America or one of the British Caribbean islands at grossly inflated prices. A young man spat at a file of infantry soldiers marching past. 'Traitors! Cowards!' he shouted. 'Go and fight the enemy!' An elderly lady dressed in tattered and stained silks wandered aimlessly to and fro, eyes glazed and muttering as though to some unseen companion. A ragged boy of perhaps ten years of age went from table to table dragging behind him his younger sister and holding out his hand for alms. As he felt in a pocket for a few coins, Keene asked him where his parents were. 'Gone, sir,' the lad replied and before he moved on he crossed himself.

'These people are really suffering,' Cutt remarked inadequately.

'Their whole world has fallen apart,' Keene said. 'For years, decades, they've lived off the fat of the land, lords and ladies in their own little utopia, like gaudy, overfed parakeets in an aviary. Now the cage has been broken open and they're at large in the real world, quite unable

122

to understand why the drab sparrows and jackdaws are attacking them.'

'You think they deserve to be hounded by slaves and savages?' Cutt wore the puzzled frown of the unthinking traditionalist for whom the created order with its distinctions of race and class was a given, only questioned by anarchists who, by very definition, must be either mad or wicked.

Keene steered away from a philosophical discussion which would be beyond the scope of his companion's intellect. 'Well, we've learned something already: morale is very low. None of these people can have much faith in Sonthonax. He's the man who sold them out to the slaves. I don't suppose it would be difficult to find a group of malcontents who'd be prepared to betray the town to Williamson.'

'You're right!' Cutt said, admiring what to him seemed to be a brilliant and original piece of deduction. 'What we need to do is get some dissident citizens together and work out a plan.'

Keene laid a restraining hand on the other man's arm. 'Not so fast! We need to know a lot more about the situation before we risk showing our hand to anyone.'

By seven o'clock the traffic to and from the town had built up to a steady cavalcade of pedestrians, wagons and horsemen. Keene decided that it was now safe to make a move. He and Cutt joined the queue passing under the languid scrutiny of sentries in the blue and white uniform that had become so familiar to Keene during the weeks of summer terror when every soldier presented a potential threat. The demeanour of these colonial guardians could scarcely have been more different. Unlike the heavily moustachioed braggarts of Paris, who sought every opportunity to display their Revolutionary zeal, the men of the Saint Domingue garrison were clean shaven, good natured and relaxed.

At the gate a sergeant demanded their papers. Keene explained that they had been driven from their homes with no time to rescue documents which could prove their

identity. Anxiously he watched the Frenchman's reaction.
The man showed neither suspicion nor surprise. 'Where are
you from?' he asked. 'Near Gonaives,' Keene replied. The
sergeant shook his head sympathetically. 'There are several
people here from that region. You'll know Citizen Constant
and Citizen Foulangère, of course.'

'They're here?' Keene improvised. 'Thank God they're
safe.'

'You'll find them in the Rue St Antoine. Ask at the Café
d'Orée. Good luck, Citizens.' He waved them through.

'That was easy,' Cutt muttered as they strolled down a
wide, straight boulevard flanked by palms.

'Don't drop your guard,' the younger man insisted. 'We
were fortunate that he didn't ask us any questions about
Gonaives. To me it's only a name on a map. For Heaven's
sake don't let yourself get drawn into any conversation about
life on the plantations.'

They devoted a couple of hours to wandering the town
and forming general impressions. The air of despondency
was almost tangible. Men and women wandered in apparent
aimlessness or sat on verandas engaged in desultory conversation. The visitors noted the high prices being asked
in the food markets and the stalls where shabbily dressed
vendors were offering for sale trinkets and finery that had
once marked them out as people of taste and refinement.
Twice they were accosted by hollow-eyed men proffer-
ing small items of jewellery, who, when refused, shuffled
away, hunch-backed with resignation. They toured the walls
and located the army barracks. The soldiers detailed to
guard duties were well turned out and seemed to be effectively disciplined. The Englishmen stood in the shade of a
jacaranda and watched a troop being drilled in musketry.
The sergeant, an aggressive little man sporting a very
wide tricolour sash, kept up a stream of invective and
imaginative insult. His charges were, if passers-by were
to believe him, a rabble of secret blank royalists, who had
only volunteered because they wanted free blank food, and

would run away at the first sign of blank danger. Well, he would make blank soldiers of them and they would defend the republic with their miserable blank lives or, by blank, he would personally shoot the cowardly, blank, blank riff-raff.

Cutt turned away with a laugh. 'I doubt General Williamson has much to fear from these fellows,' he observed.

Keene agreed. 'Not if it comes to hand-to-hand fighting but they'll be bold enough as long as they can fire from the safety of the town walls. What we need to know is the size of the garrison and its artillery strength. Time to split up. You take a close look at the displacement of cannon and try to get an idea of how well stocked the defenders are with ammunition.'

'Very well. What will you be doing?'

'These recruits have given me an idea. I'll see if I can make it work and meet you back here at sunset.' Keene strode away before the lieutenant could assail him with questions.

He walked briskly to the garrison headquarters and asked to see the duty officer. He was kept waiting in the guard room for more than half an hour but then a harassed major emerged from his office followed by an even more harassed brevet officer, juggling a large, untidy sheaf of papers. ' . . . every prominent place in the town centre,' the major was saying. 'No one is to be in any doubt. If these people want protection from the savages they're going to have to make sacrifices.'

The junior officer attempted to salute, dropped some of his papers, retrieved them and departed in confusion. The desk sergeant indicated Keene, and the major looked him over critically. 'I can give you five minutes,' he muttered and turned back into the office. 'Well?' he enquired, seating himself behind a littered desk.

Keene introduced himself. 'Georges Chêne, sometime lieutenant in the Hussars de Chamborant.'

The officer scowled. 'You mean the Second Regiment of

the People's Hussars. Aristocratic titles have been abolished. Perhaps you haven't heard that out here.'

'My apologies, Major . . . .?'

'Briand,' the soldier barked.

'My apologies, Major Briand. Old habits die hard. I thought you might be able to use the services of an experienced officer.'

The older man grunted. 'Huh, I suppose you were one of the cavalrymen who deserted on the outbreak of the Revolution.'

Keene recognised the age-old prejudice of the foot soldier against his mounted equivalent, a prejudice reinforced by the fact that several high-born cavalry officers had refused to serve the new regime. 'No, sir, I resigned my commission four years ago when my father died. I returned here then to take over the running of my family's plantation.'

'And I suppose now that you've lost your land and your slaves you suddenly find yourself in need of food and lodging.'

'I want to see this colony restored to law and order for the benefit of its people and France. It's clear to anyone with a military training that your garrison is under strength and demoralised by this slave revolt.' Keene watched with satisfaction as the officer's face reddened in anger. High emotion not infrequently loosened tongues.

But Briand soon brought his feelings under control. He sat back in his chair and a smile spread over his broad features as he said, 'I see nothing evades the eye of the cavalryman. We are, indeed, down to about half our proper garrison complement. This has been a bad year for fever and you will know that the traitors, Brandicourt and Pacot, took their men over to the enemy.'

'Cowards!' Keene snorted indignantly.

The major nodded. 'Men with no stomach for the kind of warfare we're faced with here. This black man posing as a military leader knows nothing about pitched battles. Your cavalry training will do you no good in the hills. No dashing charges with drawn sabres. This man raids out of the forest to assault poorly defended settlements and small military units, then retreats quickly before there's any chance for a counter-attack. Our one advantage is time. This Toussaint lacks the experience and the firepower to sustain a siege. His authority would soon collapse if he started throwing his ill-armed mob against our artillery.'

'So your plan is to sit it out?'

'If France keeps us supplied by sea, Port au Prince can survive indefinitely. We have outposts in the hills to keep a watch on enemy movements. We'll have good warning of any large-scale massing of soldiers, so you and your friends are quite safe in Port au Prince.'

'What about the British?'

Briand laughed. 'Old Williamson and his gallant band? The man's a veritable Don Quixote and his army is as badly afflicted by disease as ours. However,' his tone became brisk once more, 'I don't have time to discuss strategy with civilians. You want to see some action? Very well. I've a patrol going out within the hour. You can join them.'

Keene realised he was being outmanoeuvred. 'I'm afraid I couldn't take up my duties imm—'

The major stood up. 'Oh no, we don't do soldiering by convenience here. That may be the way the hussars behave but if you're going to be an infantryman you'll have to learn that it's a full-time occupation – and one that starts now. Sergeant!' he bellowed.

The duty NCO appeared in the doorway.

'M. Chêne will be accompanying the patrol to Outpost Three. See that he is equipped,' Briand ordered. He directed himself to Keene again. 'It's a two-hour march – *on foot* – into the hills. You will be escorting the new guard going out to relieve the men who've been there for a week. Then you will escort the old guard back again – *on foot*. You will return by nightfall. Then we shall see whether you have the makings of an infantry officer.'

Shortly afterwards, as he left the barracks with a file of

twenty men, under the command of Sergeant Malinaux, the foul-mouthed NCO he had earlier watched putting volunteers through their paces, Keene kept a watch for Cutt, but there was no sign of the red-headed lieutenant.

It was now the hottest part of the day and the soldiers' boots stirred the dust into white clouds. Keene had tied a kerchief round his mouth but still his tongue was dry and his nose irritated by the powdery air. Their route took them along tracks which crossed the plain before undulating over wooded foothills. The stands of mahogany and guayacan provided welcome shade from the glare of the sun but there was no respite from the energy-sapping humidity nor from the mosquitoes which clustered round the men's sweating necks and faces. Keene was glad that he was travelling light compared with the soldiers who marched in full uniform and carried knapsacks as well as their weapons.

He tried to make conversation with some of his companions but no one had effort to spare for talking. Even the voluble Sergeant Malinaux trudged silently at the head of the column, content to turn occasionally to glare his contempt for his subordinates. He set a steady, relentless pace and permitted no variation. There were no stops for rest and the men had to drink from their canteens while on the march. By the time he had been walking for an hour and a half a kind of numbness had overcome Keene's limbs. He moved with mechanical efficiency like an automaton on some great German church clock.

The column had just toiled to the top of a steeper than usual ridge when there was a sudden commotion. Shouts. Screams. The unmistakeable crackle of gunfire.

'Take cover!' Malinaux yelled.

In scrambling confusion the soldiers dived in among the trees.

Keene slithered down a slope among thick vegetation and threw himself to the ground. Splinters flew from a tree trunk above his head as a musket ball struck it and glanced off, whining, into the forest. Rapidly he primed his own piece and peered cautiously between fronds of lush fern. The initial fusillade had stopped. From his position he could make out a couple of blue-uniformed figures lying prone beside the track. Of the ambushers there was no sign.

Then a half-naked black figure appeared directly ahead, wildly brandishing what looked like a naval cutlass. Keene took careful aim and squeezed the trigger. For a long moment the rebel seemed to freeze in mid-stride, then he collapsed silently and disappeared from view. Within seconds a wailing roar went up and reverberated among the trees – a chilling, primeval yowling that crescendoed as a wave of dark-skinned warriors burst from cover. It was met by desultory shooting from the soldiers scattered in the undergrowth.

Suddenly a lone voice made itself heard above the chaos. 'Stop firing! Stop firing!' Keene saw Sergeant Malinaux step from behind a tall clump of fern, waving his musket, to which was tied a white cloth.

Eleven

There were about thirty rebels, all black except for the leader, who wore the uniform of a Spanish infantry captain but who, Keene later discovered, was in fact a French royalist who had deserted his regiment and sold his sword to the governor of Santo Domingo. The brief skirmish had cost six lives, three on each side, and the rebel leader set his captives to digging graves. Hacking at the baked earth was exhausting work, rendered even less palatable by the negroes who stood in a circle round the labourers, laughing at them and striking out with the stocks of their muskets whenever they thought someone was slacking. How they must relish this role reversal, Keene reflected: the black man become the overseer and the white man his helpless slave.

At last the work was done and preparations to march were immediately set in hand. The prisoners were attached to a long rope which passed from front to rear of the column. Then, flanked by the victors whose bare legs almost danced over the inhospitable terrain, they made their way deeper into the hill country.

The journey lasted all that day and most of the next. At night the captives were fed with raw fruit and a very passable chicken broth before being obliged to lie down beside a camp fire to sleep as best they could without any covering. The following morning the column was on the trail again before dawn and walked at a punishing pace throughout the hours of daylight. The blacks, Keene observed, were strong and muscular. They moved barefoot and lightly clad with an easy, almost an eager, grace, unlike their white companions, who made increasingly heavy weather of the forced march. From time to time the ex-slaves burst into rhythmical song. Though their language was basically French, it was freely mingled with dialect words and pronounced with such a rough accent that Keene could not understand it. However their laughter, gestures and glances left little doubt that the impromptu librettos were all at the expense of the prisoners.

Their destination was a large plantation on the country's central plateau. The column passed a perimeter post where, Keene noticed, white sentries, still in the blue and white uniforms of the French army, mounted a guard that gave every appearance of being efficient and disciplined. A long, straight drive led up to the residence, a large, single-storey building in white stone. Around it a wide area of land once planted with coffee had been cleared to provide a space for scores of thatched huts. Smoke rose from numerous cooking fires tended by black women, whose children and menfolk wandered around freely paying little attention to the new arrivals.

Beyond the house a different kind of camp came into view. Here there were tents and wooden huts laid out in straight lines. Clearly these were the quarters assigned to the French troops who had defected to Toussaint's side. What sort of a man, Keene wondered, could command the devotion – or, at least, the obedience – of a racially divided army? Could there be any cohesion in such a rag-tag assembly? Could Toussaint's power base have any permanent stability? Could it only survive in the unique circumstances currently prevailing in Saint Domingue? As long as the ex-slaves were intoxicated with the heady wine of freedom and the renegade troops had licence to loot and plunder, their leader might count on their support but, sooner or later, the task would be laid upon him of rebuilding a shattered economy and creating a sound polity. Few generals that Keene knew of from his extensive reading had ever mastered the arts of peaceful governance. For weeks he had been curious to meet this strange phenomenon. The closer he came to the man the stronger was his desire.

The prisoners were escorted to their accommodation, a long wooden building with one door, no windows and an earth floor sparsely scattered with straw. 'Is this Toussaint's headquarters?' Keene asked the captain as they were roughly pushed inside. 'You'll find out tomorrow,' was the surly reply with which he had to be content.

In the morning Keene and his companions were escorted to the bank of a small stream a hundred yards from their lodging and ordered to wash, shave and generally make themselves respectable enough to be paraded before the *maréchal de camp*. After this they were fed a kind of tasteless maize gruel before being formed up in two ranks in front of their hut. An officer then inspected them minutely, ordering one man to fall out and burnish his buttons, another to repair a tear in his jacket, a third to brush the dust from his wide-brimmed hat. 'Smarten yourselves up, all of you!' he roared. 'I'm not taking a bunch of scruffs like you before the *maréchal*.'

When the martinet reluctantly declared himself satisfied with his charges they were once again formed up in two files and marched to the house. They came to a halt in the wide drive before the arcaded front and there they waited. And waited. And waited. The men's long shadows steadily shrank before them as they stood for what seemed several hours, trying not to shuffle or gaze around. Every detected movement was punished with a hefty blow from the butt of an NCO's musket.

Then, suddenly, he was there. The front door opened and a small group of senior officers descended the shallow steps. Keene's first sighting of Toussaint l'Ouverture prompted mixed reactions. The conqueror of Saint Domingue was small and very black but there was nothing in the least insignificant about him. His impact was partly achieved by the splendour of his dress. His stature was enhanced by his hat, a tall bicorn surmounted by an elaborate white plume.

The green coat topping immaculate white breeches was heavily embroidered with gold thread, particularly around the collar, and Toussaint's shoulders were 'squared off' with deep epaulettes. But this military leader had no need of accoutrements. He possessed that 'presence' which no tailor can manufacture and no tutor teach. It preceded him like a wave as he detached himself from his entourage and sauntered towards his prisoners. When he spoke it was in the careful French of a self-educated man, and Keene, who had also known a childhood innocent of book learning, felt a strange parallelism with the little tyrant.

'Men of France,' Toussaint began, and as he spoke the wide gap in his row of gleaming white teeth had an almost hypnotic attraction, 'I address you as a fellow subject of the king and as the representative of the king in this colony. It is my intention, with the aid of my Spanish allies, to restore Saint Domingue to its Bourbon allegiance and to make of it a land of free men under the crown. The greater part of the territory is already under my control, and most of the soldiers who had been enticed away from their duty by Jacobin rhetoric and the promise of a spurious liberty have responded to my offer of a free pardon. That offer I now extend to you. I remind you of the oath that, until recent lamentable events, all soldiers swore on their enlistment – "to king and country unto death". I do not ask you to change your allegiance but to return to your true allegiance. But I place no pressure on any of you. You each have a choice, either to come and fight with us in a holy cause or to remain prisoners for the duration of the war. If you choose the latter you have my word that you will be honourably treated. However, I trust that, like loyal Frenchman, you will grasp this opportunity to restore order in Saint Domingue and to play a part in restoring order to France. I shall now demand a decision of each one of you in turn.'

Having delivered himself of that brief oration, Toussaint walked across to the prisoners and went along the ranks asking each man's name and posing the question, 'Are you with us or with the rebels?' Of course, there was not a single individual who elected to spend months or perhaps years in a fever-ridden jail rather than take his chance under the leadership of the black man.

Keene had only a couple of minutes to decide on his own response. In recent weeks he'd pledged himself, by turns, to his own independence, to Challoner's information service, to Hamilton's autocratic vision for America and to Genet's international republicanism. Was he to play the chameleon yet again? He certainly had no desire to end his days fighting an obscure war in the tropical jungle of a remote French colony, nor to find himself held a perpetual prisoner in this white man's graveyard.

Now the diminutive negro with the oversize head was in front of him, looking him up and down with a quizzical stare. *'Et vous, Monsieur? Vous êtes planteur?'*

Keene looked down into the searching brown eyes and replied in precise French, 'I am George Keene, representative of his Majesty George III, King of Great Britain and all her overseas territories.'

Toussaint took a step backwards, eyebrows raised in astonishment. *'Vraiment?'*

'Certainly. His Majesty has heard of your brave exploits and your stand against the Revolutionary rabble and wishes to open direct diplomatic relations with you.' Keene adopted a pose of courteous formality befitting the words and watched, anxiously, for the other man's response. Toussaint might well be sceptical about a royal emissary arriving in so unorthodox a fashion but, Keene reasoned, the very possibility of an official approach from London was so flattering that the slave leader, desperate for recognition, could surely not afford to reject it.

With a nod and grunt Toussaint moved on thoughtfully down the line. Keene was aware of murmuring among his companions – murmuring that was far from friendly. He did not relish the prospect of being returned to their shared quarters with a group of burly French soldiers, hostile to Britain and angry at having been duped.

The inspection over, Toussaint spoke briefly to the parade officer, then turned with his escort to remount the steps of his residence. The fierce officer faced his charges and ordered them to 'right turn'. Keene's heart sank. The ruse had failed and he had condemned himself, at the very least, to a savage battering from Malinaux and his men. The officer strutted along the line. When he reached Keene he stopped. 'You,' he muttered, with a sneer of contempt, 'fall out and await further orders.' Keene stepped away from the column. The command 'Forward march' was given and the latest batch of new recruits to Toussaint l'Ouverture's army were led away to assume their duties.

The Englishman felt the heat of the climbing sun on his neck and shoulders as he stood, alone, in the empty space before the house. Members of the black *maréchal*'s following went about their varied business and paid him little attention as the long minutes passed. But any indication that he was being ignored was an illusion as Keene knew whenever he glanced across at the house. Several of the windows were still unshuttered and thrown open to allow the cooler morning airs to blow through the rooms. In the space framed by one to the right of the main door he caught occasional glimpses of the general and his suite pacing to and fro within. Sometimes they stared in his direction. It was not difficult to guess the subject of their conversation.

Keene sensed that it would be discourteous to take out his watch in order to discover how long he was being kept waiting. If he were to act the diplomat he must assume the diplomat's professional clothing of patience, respect and unshakeable tranquillity. He judged that some twenty minutes had passed before one of Toussaint's Spanish aides emerged to convey him into the great man's presence.

The general sat upright on an elaborate sofa covered in faded silk of the fashion prevailing in Paris some thirty years earlier. The incongruity struck Keene immediately.

Here was a member of an inferior race, a poor black, placing his backside upon a luxury item created by sweated industry in the atelier of a leading ebeniste for the comfort of some modish grande dame whose family had grown rich on the products of slave labour.

Keene smiled and made a formal bow. 'It is good of your excellency to receive me,' he said. Toussaint waved his guest to a fauteuil and, for some moments, scrutinised him in silence. Behind him stood three senior officers, two Spanish and one French, and it was clear from the expressions on their faces that they had little taste for this interview.

'Your approach is very unconventional,' Toussaint observed eventually.

'I beg your Excellency's pardon,' Keene said, modelling his erect posture on his host's. 'Your military headquarters are difficult to locate.'

'How is it that you "locate" our camp in the company of enemy troops?' one of the Spaniards wanted to know.

'By happy chance,' Keene explained. 'My ship, HMS *Promise*, set me ashore, as arranged, close to the British encampment, where I hoped to gain intelligence as to your Excellency's whereabouts. However, you have been so successful in concealing your plans that Major General Williamson's staff was unable to offer me any real assistance. My only hope of finding your Excellency, therefore, lay with the French. Hence my subterfuge of posing as a dispossessed planter seeking a military employment. I hoped that by mingling with men who had engaged your forces in battle I might gain some idea of where to conduct my search. In the event, your men surprised our patrol and saved me the effort.'

'You must be a new breed of diplomat,' the Frenchman suggested scornfully. 'I've never yet met one prepared to hazard his life in the cause of international relations.'

With only the hint of a smile, Keene riposted, 'Perhaps, sir, it has been your misfortune only to encounter French diplomats.' To Toussaint he added, 'His Britannic Majesty is anxious, as a matter of the utmost urgency, to regularise relations between our two nations and to assure you that we are as committed as our Spanish allies to assisting you in your struggle against anti-royalist forces.'

'You have letters from his Majesty?' The *maréchal's* dark eyes revealed little but he leaned forward, eager Keene guessed, for some tangible connection with his 'brother' monarch in London.

Keene had to bluff. 'All my papers and credentials are aboard the *Promise*,' he said. 'I could not risk them being discovered on my person by the French.'

One of the aides snorted in disbelief but Toussaint nodded sagely. 'We will make arrangements to collect them. Meanwhile, what does King George propose?'

'He offers ships, men and munitions to help you complete your conquest of Saint Domingue.'

'My Spanish allies have been generous in their support.'

'Yet Port au Prince and the southern region lie outside your control and you will need a large land and sea force to take the capital.'

'You are singularly well informed, Mr Keene,' one of the Spaniards commented dryly. 'We all know the covetous eyes Britain has cast upon this colony—'

Toussaint held up a hand to silence him. 'What progress is the anti-slave-trade legislation making through your parliament, Mr Keene?'

So, the Englishman thought, this little man from the West Indian plantations knows about the efforts of William Wilberforce and his libertarian colleagues. Did he also know that Pitt's initial support for his friend had cooled since the outbreak of the war against social radicalism? 'The movers of the bill have the support of the Prime Minister. I have no doubt they will prevail over the mercantile interest in what is a matter of high principle.'

'Ah, but when, Mr Keene, when? Do you think abolition of the trade in my people and the end of slavery itself is at all close at hand?' The negro watched closely for Keene's response.

The Englishman's brain whirled. How would a diplomat respond, he considered; appearing to promise everything but, in fact, conceding nothing. 'His Majesty is aware of the abominable treatment meted out to your people in Saint Domingue—'

'And in his own colonies,' Toussaint interrupted.

Keene nodded. 'And in *some* places of his Majesty's dominions at the outermost reaches of his compassionate authority. Any understanding between our countries would certainly have at its heart the well-being of black populations.'

'And their independence?'

'Should I report to his Majesty that that is a condition of the establishment of full fraternal relations with your Excellency?'

The general stood up and Keene followed suit. 'My first responsibility is to my people,' the black man said imperiously. 'My second is to my allies. It is not always easy to balance them.' He walked to a side table, picked up a little silver bell and rang it – a custom, Keene surmised, learned from the colonial master race Toussaint so roundly despised. A servant appeared almost immediately.

'This man will convey you to your new quarters,' the *maréchal* explained. 'He will also seek out for you a suitable change of apparel. Please feel free to come and go as you please within the compound. We will have further discussions when I have given your words careful consideration.'

Keene's room at one end of the long building was a distinct improvement on his more recent accommodation and on his cramped berth aboard the *Promise*. The clothes brought to him, although a little short for complete comfort, were of high-quality linen, brocade and velvet – doubtless from the wardrobe of the plantation owner ousted by Toussaint's soldiery and, perhaps, now thrown upon the charity of some community in Virginia or the Carolinas.

When he had washed the sweat from his face and neck he went out into the compound. He discovered that what had once been an extensive plantation was now wholly given over to the needs of Toussaint's piebald army. Whites and blacks were clearly segregated, though whether by diktat or mutual choice was not clear. Only some of the negro women, plying their ancient trade, passed easily between the two communities. Methodically, Keene observed and stored away for future use everything of significance. A large parade-ground area had been cleared and squads of Toussaint's barefoot black infantry were sending up clouds of dust as they were drilled by white NCOs. They lacked the precision of English or French grenadiers but they were well disciplined and what they lacked in polish they more than made up for in enthusiasm, energy and stamina. These men who had been torn from their African homelands for long, backbreaking service in the plantations made powerful, strong soldiers. It would be a foolish enemy commander who underestimated their effectiveness.

Beyond the central area given over to purely military purposes the hills and valleys were dotted with clusters of mud and thatch huts, 'village' communes where Toussaint's camp followers and married troops had settled their families. Plots of ground had been cleared for the growth of simple crops and the penning of chickens, sheep and goats. Here and there forlorn clumps of coffee bushes were evidence of a forsaken cash-crop agriculture and the adjacent forest bore the scars of trees felled for construction or firewood. Keene tried to estimate the number of men under Toussaint's command. Three thousand? Five thousand? More in other encampments round the country. Here was an army who knew the terrain and could live simply off the land for years, perhaps for generations if necessary. Given effective leadership they would never be dislodged by whole contingents of Europe's finest soldiers fighting in alien conditions against heat, fever and a formidable foe.

That evening, as the brief tropical dusk was yielding to

a balmy night alive with the noises of crickets and buzzing insects, Keene was summoned to dine with the *maréchal* and his staff. He found himself seated at Toussaint's right at one end of a long mahogany table whose polished surface reflected the light from candles set in ornate silver candelabra. The all-male company ate from porcelain bearing the monogram 'ED', which, it transpired from the conversation, stood for Etienne Dubois, the departed owner of all these fineries. 'Dubois', Keene reflected; a common name, conveying no hint of aristocratic connections. Yet, here this family of inauspicious origins had lived like lords, their estate manned by thousands of black serfs, their irresistibly mounting profits enabling them to afford luxuries that few of their countrymen could aspire to. Perhaps they had already been counting the days to the time that they could put a manager into the running of the plantation, return to France, buy land, a spectacular chateau and a residence *'en ville'*, and marry into the *real* aristocracy. Keene pictured the men and women of his imaginary family seated round this table, discussing the alarming news from home and regretfully concluding that their dreams must await fulfilment till the dreadful republicans in Paris had been 'dealt with'. How stunned they must have been when their ideal world had been destroyed, not by military invasion but by the unsuspected weevil within.

The negro presided with the grace of an accomplished host and Keene guessed that he must have spent many years in a sophisticated household carefully observing the niceties of the white man's etiquette. Talk traversed issues of general interest – the war in Europe, government changes in Paris, the political situation in England, the problems of seaborne commerce. Keene tried to do more listening than speaking but Toussaint obviously relished having at his table someone with a fresh viewpoint and questioned him closely. However, nothing of real substance was discussed until after the meal, when the company removed to a spacious salon where groups of men clustered in conversational islands to relax in armchairs and drink rum. Toussaint drew Keene to a corner table. He spoke with the combination of urgency and confidentiality of a man who seeks to explain things to himself as much as to his hearer.

'Mr Keene, you must understand that I cannot enter into an alliance with any nation that does not guarantee the liberty of all black people.'

The 'diplomat' weighed his response carefully. 'His Majesty and his Majesty's ministers are somewhat surprised – though, of course, gratified – that your Excellency has not entered upon a concordat with Governor Sonthonax. I understand that he has announced the liberty of all slaves in Saint Domingue.'

'Pah! Sonthonax is a palm tree; he bends to the prevailing wind. When the tempest that is Toussaint l'Ouverture burst upon him he was quick to become the black man's friend. But what did he do as soon as some of my people foolishly laid down their arms? He sent them back to their old masters. In any case Sonthonax does not speak for France. In France the "aristocracy of the skin" still prevails.'

'There are many who oppose it – and not only in France. I know of many in Britain who have renounced coffee because it is a crop watered with the blood of your people.'

Momentary anger blazed in the negro's eyes. 'And for the fastidiousness of a few genteel English men and ladies salving their own consciences I should be grateful? No, Mr Keene, it will take more than gestures – however sincerely meant – to move governments and the commercial interests who support them.'

Keene faced up to the *maréchal*'s indignation. 'Then, I am to return your Excellency's answer that an understanding between our two governments is not deemed to be in your Excellency's interests?'

Toussaint was silent for several moments. When he spoke again it was with wistful humour. 'What do they say of Toussaint l'Ouverture in the salons and coffee houses of

London? That he is a flash in the pan, an aberration, an uncultured savage whose movement cannot possibly last?'

'If there are any who hold such views I am now in a position to disabuse them. It will be my pleasant responsibility to inform his Majesty that in Toussaint l'Ouverture he has a potential ally who should be assisted to establish a secure government in Saint Domingue and with whom mutually beneficial commercial ties should be established.'

The *maréchal* shook his head. 'Tell him rather that Toussaint l'Ouverture is the hammer of God, divinely appointed to right the ancient wrongs visited upon his people by generations of Frenchmen, Englishmen and Spaniards. Say that I offer him a place at my side in the international crusade against injustice and oppression.' The man's eyes were glinting with passion. 'It is the same offer I make to all governments. Only two days ago I despatched envoys to Paris challenging the Convention to decide what it means by "liberty" and "brotherhood". Those ideals are not divisible. They apply to all men or they apply to none.' He paused, then with a disarming smile added, 'I shall write these things in a letter and you shall deliver it to King George.'

While Keene's head was still ringing with this extraordinary oration, the black leader stood. Every man in the room sprang to his feet and Toussaint, with grave nods to right and left, walked calmly through the salon.

Keene had no further meetings with this remarkable man. Two days later he was woken with the news that the *maréchal* had departed on campaign but had left instructions that his guest was to be furnished with letters for King George and Mr Pitt and escorted safely to the coast.

JERVIS

'A man of extraordinary force of mind and character . . . far from always preserving an unruffled command of his temper or of himself . . . '

Joseph Tucker

Twelve

The journey down from the plateau was much easier than the ascent. Keene's small party was provided with horses, and though their sweat attracted the attention of swarms of flies and mosquitoes they made travel along forest tracks much less wearisome. Twenty-four hours after leaving Toussaint's camp the riders had their first glimpse of the sea.

Keene's anxieties were far from over. He had been six days away from the *Promise* and there was no way of knowing whether she would still be at Petit Goeve. Hawkestone would, of course, wait as long as he could and would use every endeavour to locate his friend. Keene imagined with some amusement the rating 'Razor' Cutt would receive on confessing that he had 'lost' his charge. Yet, in reality, there was little that the captain could do to find him and he would, eventually, be forced to resume his progress to Barbados.

If the frigate was still in harbour, Keene still had one other problem to deal with – his credibility. The escort provided by Toussaint was under the command of one of his most trusted aides, a mulatto called Vernet. He was under orders to receive from Keene the documents supposedly entrusted by King George to his 'emissary' for delivery to his 'ally' in Saint Domingue. Keene might secure his own safety but there seemed no way of preventing Toussaint realising that he had been tricked. The blow to his pride would be immense and the chances of his ever trusting a real embassy from London remote. Keene reflected ruefully on the fraud he had perpetrated for his own preservation and the consequences it might have for government policy.

His first concern became a reality when the group emerged from a belt of trees above the harbour. They now had a clear view of the anchorage. It was empty. He lifted his eyes towards the waters of the bay beyond, hoping against hope for some sight of the frigate. Was that a vessel under half sail in the shadow of the distant headland? He strained his eyes to see. Yes, there was a ship there. It emerged now into the full sunlight a mile, perhaps a mile and a half, offshore and heading seaward. Now its lines became more distinct, the unmistakeable lines of a British warship. It had to be the *Promise*.

Keene turned to Vernet, pointing agitatedly to the departing vessel. 'Quick!' he yelled. 'A musket!'

Grasping the situation, the mulatto handed over his weapon, ready primed. Keene raised it above his head and fired. His companions responded excitedly. Volley after volley cracked in the still air. Keene spurred his horse to the summit of the hill, standing in the stirrups and furiously waving the firearm above his head. Would Hawkestone hear the commotion over the noises of a ship leaving harbour? Would he train his telescope on the shore?

Anxiously Keene watched as the *Promise* slid steadily away from the land. There was no sign of her progress being halted. Now Keene looked down again at Petit Goeve. With escape so close he could not give up. There must be a fishing boat or some other small craft that Vernet could commandeer. The chances of overhauling a three-masted naval vessel built for speed and manoeuvrability were small but Hawkestone was unsure of the coastal waters and would proceed cautiously. It might just be possible . . .

One of Vernet's men shouted something and pointed with a broad grin on his face. Keene stared once more at the distant *Promise*. What was the excited fellow yelling in his thick patois? Keene could see no change in the frigate's direction. Then, suddenly, he realised what the negro's sharp eyes had detected: Hawkestone was taking in sail. The canvas of the mainmast diminished in areas as main and tops were furled. Simultaneously, he saw a puff of smoke from the frigate's side, followed instantly by the crash of one of her twelve-pounders. As the watchers kept their eyes fixed on the English ship they saw a boat pull away from its stern and head, with steady strokes, in their direction.

'We'd better stay here, in full view,' Keene said to Vernet. 'They can land on the beach below us.' He indicated the narrow shingle at the foot of the steep gradient falling away from their present position.

The horsemen dismounted and allowed their animals to crop leaves from the bushes close to the cliff top. Keene peered over the edge at the scramble of loose rock and vegetation and a simple plan took shape in his mind. He waited till the boat was some hundred yards from the shore. He could see Sam Cutt standing in the stern, urging the rowers onward. He noted, with satisfaction, that the lieutenant was holding a pistol in case of trouble.

Keene turned to the mulatto. 'They may suspect a trap,' he said. 'I must go and assure them that you are friends.'

Without waiting for a reply he clambered over the cliff edge and began his slithering descent. It was hazardous. He half ran, half fell, grabbing wildly at bushes growing out of the rock face as his feet slipped and stumbled on the shifting scree. It was difficult to time his arrival on the thin strip of beach, yet timing was vital. He steadied himself some twenty feet from the bottom and assessed the situation. The boatmen were shipping oars as their craft reached shallow water. Keene was now out of sight of the watchers above. He waited until the seamen were jumping over the side, some steadying the boat, others wading ashore. Then in three strides he jumped the remaining slope, at the same time letting out a sharp cry of pain. He threw himself on to the shingle and lay in a crumpled heap, very still.

Within seconds sea boots scrunched the stones behind him. 'Mr Keene! Mr Keene! Are you injured?'

The escapee looked up into Sam Cutt's anxious face and smiled.

'Thank the Lord, sir. I thought—'

'Save your gratitude, Cutt!' Keene said sharply. 'I'm unconscious. You understand? Unconscious and injured. I must be carried to the boat quickly and got away before the men up there know what's happening.'

The lieutenant hesitated. 'I don't—'

'Now, Cutt! Now!'

The officer snapped out orders and Keene felt himself hoisted up by two sailors. He allowed his arms to hang limply down as they rushed him to the waiting longboat.

As he was placed on the wet timbers and the craft slithered off the pebbles to float free, Keene heard distant shouts. 'Ignore 'em, Cutt,' he muttered. 'Get us back to the *Promise* double quick!'

He heard the splash of oars in the water. He heard another sound – the crackle of musket fire.

'They're shooting at us, Mr Keene,' the lieutenant commented, unnecessarily.

'Give 'em a couple of rounds with your pistol – but be sure not to hit anyone.'

The boat jerked forward as the sailors bent to their task. There were shouts from the land and more desultory firing, returned by Cutt. A ball rattled the gunwale close to Keene's ear. One of the men yelled an expletive and held a hand to his shoulder, missing his stroke. With a grimace he retrieved his oar and went on rowing. Gradually the sounds of angry pursuit were drowned by the creaking of the rowlocks and the lapping of wavelets.

After a couple of minutes Keene asked from his recumbent position, 'What are they doing now?'

'Standing at the shoreline waving,' said Cutt. 'They don't look too happy.'

Keene smiled up at him. 'Well done, Sam. A smart piece

of work. Now listen carefully. This is our story – for Captain Hawkestone and anyone else who wants to know. You found me knocked senseless at the bottom of the cliff. I'd taken a bad tumble. You naturally wanted to get me to the ship's doctor without delay. When my companions back there started shouting and firing you assumed they wanted to recapture me, so you ordered your men to redouble their efforts. You had no means of knowing that the fellows with me were friends and, since I was silenced and, for all you knew, near to death, you had no means of checking the facts. You took the initiative and acted in all respects as a resourceful and responsible officer.' He looked around at the sailors closest to him. 'There's half a guinea for every man as sticks to that story come hell or high water.'

Cutt nodded solemnly. The others laughed. Someone called out, 'We're your men, Mr Keene!'

Aboard the frigate Keene allowed himself to be laid on the cot in his cabin. He made no response when first Hawkestone, then the ship's surgeon came to look at him. He heard the rhythmic tramp of feet on the deck as men worked the capstan and the rattling of unfurled sails descending the mast. Soon he felt the familiar motion of a ship under way. Only then, with a groan, did he open his eyes and stage a return to consciousness.

Whether Hawkestone believed the story he spun, Keene could not say. The doctor announced that his patient showed no signs of internal or external injury but pronounced his professional opinion that 'a man's head is a strange beast, given to unaccountable humours'. In his opinion Keene had suffered temporary loss of consciousness due to shock. The captain declared himself satisfied with this verdict while at the same time giving his friend the occasional quizzical glance which hinted, 'You and I both know there's more to this business than you're saying but if you want to keep your secrets, so be it.'

Later, when they were in the great cabin and Keene was trying to look languid and not eat too hearty a dinner, he gave Hawkestone a censored version of his recent adventure. After the captain had explained, apologetically, that he had waited as long as he could for M. Chêne's return and sent out frequent reconnaissance parties in the hope of finding news of his whereabouts, he asked, 'What do you make of him, then, this black fellow?'

'A man not to be underestimated,' was Keene's immediate response.

'You don't suppose he'll last long, do you? These ignorant demagogues rise and fall like . . .' Hawkestone racked his brain for a suitable simile, 'like the beams of Mr Newcomen's steam engines.'

Keene looked thoughtful. 'The steam that drives this particular engine is a formidable force. Toussaint has a fierce idealism. He told me, with great fervour, that liberty is for all men or for none. Tell me, Charles, how would you respond to such a claim?'

Hawkestone drained the last of his rum. He pushed his chair away from the table before replying. 'I'd say as many sins are committed in the name of liberty as in the exercise of tyranny – perhaps more. Isn't France proof of that? Isn't that what this war is all about?'

Keene shook his head wearily. 'Heaven bless me, Charles, if I've the faintest notion what this war is about. I've looked at it from just about every angle and no two facets are the same. It'll bring about change and most men of sensibility grant that change there must be, but what the new order will look like . . .' He shrugged.

Hawkestone's worried frown returned. 'I grant you, George, that our society ain't perfect – none ever is. But, dammit man, there must be order. There'll always be people at the top and people at the bottom and people at different levels in between. That's the way God made us. Why, only last year I heard the Bishop of Salisbury say as much in a sermon when he came to Collingbourne.'

Keene gave a cynical laugh. 'So a benign God ordained some to be bishops and some to be heirs to fine Wiltshire estates and some to be nobodies – like George Keene, predestined to go about the world like the Wandering Jew, seeking an elusive destiny?'

This sudden, lashing bitterness silenced the captain and it was Keene who went on, 'Tell me, Charles, in this nicely graded social scheme of yours are there whole races designed for servitude? Does a black skin deprive a man of the rights we enjoy? I say nothing of the Caribbean slave owners or the merchant-captains who buy and sell Africans like so many head of cattle. I leave Mr Wilberforce and his friends to accuse them at the bar of humanity. But I tell you what puzzles – and sickens – me, Charles. In America they make a god of Liberty and regularly blaspheme his name with every social contract they enter into.'

'I thought you approved of America . . . planned to settle down there,' Hawkestone muttered.

'I did once. Now . . . ?'

'George, the Wandering Jew, eh?'

Keene was not to be deflected. 'Do you know, Charles, that in "the land of the free" they treat household servants in ways that would make any decent English gentleman thoroughly ashamed? Do you know they enslave, not merely immigrant Africans, but the very indigenous people of the lands they've settled? Do you know they import what they euphemistically call "contract wives" because they don't have enough women of their own? Do you know that there is worse exploitation and sheer, brutal cruelty in America than was ever practised in France by an arrogant aristocracy? And it's all excused by one simple idea – people whose skin is a different colour must, ipso facto, be inferior, no better than animals.'

Hawkestone stood up and walked to the stern window. He tried to lighten the atmosphere. 'I think, on the whole George, I prefer the Bishop of Salisbury's sermons to yours. Now, what report—'

Keene was not listening. 'I've encountered many closed minds, Charles. Time was when I thought no skull was

151

thicker or more dense than that of your average, smug, self-satisfied English milord. But I tell you there is no country in the civilised world in which independence of mind and freedom of discussion are so inhibited as in America.'

Roused now, Hawkestone walked back to the table, rested both hands upon it and glowered at his companion. 'I think you're right to be leaving Challoner's service, George. All this fraternisation with rebels and demagogues has made a revolutionary of you. Now, may I remind you that we ain't planning a war against America. We're gathering information about the state of affairs in the West Indies. I want to know all you can tell me about Saint Domingue, because in a few days' time I have to make a report to Vice Admiral Jervis.'

'Jervis?' It was a name whose fame extended far beyond the Royal Navy.

'Yes, I had the information from an incoming ship a couple of days ago. The grand old man himself is leading the expedition. Twenty capital ships, it's said, and his own flag in the *Boyne*, ninety-eight. Big business, George, and Jervis will want . . . will *demand* the very best, up-to-date intelligence. Now, I don't intend to cross him by presenting a report that's any less than perfect. He has a ferocious temper. His crews fear him much more than any enemy. And he makes and breaks captains for sport. So, if you please, George, let's have less of your philosophy and more hard fact.'

Thirteen

The *Promise* reached Barbados in the middle of January 1794. As they sailed into harbour her crew had their first sight of the great fleet sent to conquer France's West Indian colonies – twenty-seven capital ships and frigates riding sedately at anchor and dressed overall, the pride of the British navy. As the frigate came to anchor Keene gazed at the congregation of war vessels with their neatly furled sails, gleaming paintwork and pennants shifting in a light offshore breeze and could not resist a feeling of elation. Here was, surely, an irresistible fighting machine, for the Revolutionary republic had nothing comparable throughout the islands with which to match it.

The spectacle also spoke volumes about the nature of command. Within the fleet's stately calm there was evidence of fervent industry. Topmen sat astride spars splicing sheets, their feet dangling a hundred feet above the deck. Below them colleagues scrubbed timber, polished brass and renewed paintwork. Squads of marines were being put through their drill. Not a man, it seemed, was permitted to be idle. Everything was in keeping with Vice Admiral Jervis's well-known dictum that to run an efficient, trouble-free ship the basic technique was to 'keep the bastards busy'.

During the crossing from Saint Domingue, Keene had learned a great deal about Sir John Jervis, most of it from Hawkestone, who was in awe, not to say fear, of the man and whose anxiety increased with every sea mile covered. John Jervis had entered the service almost half a century before and fought his way up through the ranks. He was proud to have it known that his early years as an able seaman had been ones of extreme penury and hardship because his father, disapproving of the boy's desire to go to sea, had refused him any financial aid. When disciplining errant crewmen he could justifiably boast, 'There ain't no below-decks trick I don't know.'

From the beginning Jervis had set his sights on an admiral's flag and he pursued his goal with absolute single-mindedness. He had achieved his first command during the assault on Quebec in 1759 and had greatly impressed the ill-fated General Wolfe. Like all men driven by the demon of ambition, he was intolerant of those who could not share his dedication. Discipline aboard Jervis's vessels was rigid, rapid and rigorous. The name '*Albany*' was still whispered among disaffected seamen as a warning to watch their behaviour. It referred to an attempted mutiny in Jervis's ship which had been put down with the utmost severity a quarter of a century before and had rapidly assumed the nature of legend. Every seaborne crime was regarded as a personal affront and an offence against the nation and Jervis was not the man to shrink from ordering floggings in retribution and *pour encourager les autres*. Another story told of him with relish was his treatment of two runaway Turkish slaves who had escaped from a galley and hidden themselves in a ship's boat of the *Alarm* when he was serving on the Mediterranean station. They were subsequently captured by the local authorities but this was not good enough for the captain, who had come close to creating an international incident out of the affair. Claiming that the British flag had been insulted, he insisted on the miscreants being brought on board the *Alarm* to receive punishment and actually threatened war against the Venetian republic (in whose waters the crime had been perpetrated) if his demands were not met.

Such was the man with whom Hawkestone was about to rendezvous. A man who demanded, and therefore received, only the highest standards from his subordinates. A man who had emerged from several naval engagements with the name of 'hero' and who was only content to have heroes under his command. Hawkestone had, in recent days, checked, double-checked and triple-checked every inch of the *Promise*, above and below decks. Members of the crew exchanged glances and muttered comments at his uncharacteristic ferocity.

Now, as the two friends stood by the bowsprit, Keene observed, 'The old *Promise* is really looking her best.'

'Aye, she's not a bad little craft.' Hawkestone looked wistfully at the row of ships across the water and Keene knew that he was seeing himself, not as a young flag officer enjoying his first command, but as a naval career man very near the bottom of the post-captains' list. It was the first time Keene had understood that his friend had real ambitions.

Hawkestone had sent Cutt across to the *Boyne* with a message respectfully seeking permission to go aboard and present his compliments. Now he repeatedly trained his telescope on the mast tops of the flagship.

'What are you looking for?' Keene asked.

'Jervis's signal,' the captain replied. 'When he's ready to receive me, he'll hoist the union flag to the mizzen top, with the flag denoting *Promise*'s number in the Admiralty lists – 431.'

'Here comes Cutt back again. Perhaps he brings a message.' Keene pointed to the returning longboat.

Hawkestone shook his head. 'No, vice admirals don't engage in private correspondence with junior captains.' He handed his spyglass to a midshipman. 'Watch the *Boyne* for the signal!' he barked. 'Don't take your eyes off her. Report to me the moment our flag appears.' He marched along the deck.

The captain was partially wrong about admirals not communicating directly with lesser mortals. Lieutenant Cutt brought back a verbal message from Sir John: 'The admiral will be obliged if Captain Hawkestone will call upon him at 3 p.m. – with Mr Keene.'

Hawkestone looked severely at his subordinate. 'What did you tell the admiral about Mr Keene?'

'Nothing, Cap'n. He seemed to know all about the gentleman already.'

The source of Jervis's information rapidly became clear after their arrival aboard the *Boyne*. They were rowed across the anchorage in good time for their appointed audience and were kept waiting on the quarterdeck but at three o'clock precisely a servant came up the companionway to escort them to the admiral's day cabin, a spacious, comfortably appointed apartment extending the width of the ship's stern, with windows on three sides. There were two men in the room, Jervis, in full uniform, was seated by a bureau in one corner, and a tall figure in civilian clothes of formal cut stood by the aft window.

Keene's first impression of Sir John Jervis was that he was small but powerfully built. His keen eyes surveyed the new arrivals as he acknowledged Hawkestone's salute with a nod.

The admiral turned to his companion. 'Sir Charles Grey, may I present Captain Charles Hawkestone of the *Promise* and Mr George Keene.' He explained, 'Sir Charles is general of land forces for this expedition.'

It was a name Keene knew. Grey, now well into his sixties, was one of Britain's longest serving soldiers, an officer of the old school. It was clearly a measure of the importance attached to the West Indian campaign that commanders of such standing as Jervis and Grey had been appointed to lead it. But, Keene questioned, was it wise policy to send such veterans against the forces of Revolutionary France – forces fired with a burning vision for a better world? Modern wars, he was convinced, were not like old ones in which armies were sent out in the names of rival kings to conquer or reconquer stretches of territory. Generals and admirals now found themselves facing, not other generals and admirals who had learned their profession from the same books on tactics and strategy, but *peoples*, fighting for their livelihoods and their right to self-determination. Such combatants neither knew nor cared about the 'rules' of war and the traditional deployment of cavalry, infantry and artillery. They attacked where their foes were weakest, often in small bands capable of disappearing into their native hills and woods. They defended desperately to the last man, needing no officer-corps braggadocio to urge them to self-sacrifice. Failure to appreciate all this had cost Britain her American colonies. Yet still, it seemed, the lessons had not been learned.

'Glad to make your acquaintance, gentlemen,' the general said. 'Sir Thomas Challoner speaks highly of you both.'

So, Keene thought, it was the spymaster who had been preparing the ground for them. He calculated quickly. How much would Challoner have told them? The tight-lipped Sir Thomas never let out more information than was absolutely necessary. The answer to his question came almost immediately.

'As you know,' Jervis directed his remarks to Hawkestone, who still stood stiffly in the middle of the room, hat under one arm, 'the Admiralty operates a first-rate intelligence service. That don't mean we ain't grateful for any *reliable* news that may come our way from other sources. So, what have you discovered about the enemy's strength in the islands?'

Hawkestone gave his carefully prepared report while the two listeners nodded, grunted and asked occasional questions.

'Of course, Saint Domingue will be the easiest apple to pluck – and the juiciest,' Grey suggested. 'I gather the Frogs have a full-blown native Revolution on their hands.'

'As to that, sir,' Hawkestone said, 'I think Keene can tell you more than I.'

Both older men looked expectantly at Keene.

He decided there was no point in being anything other than frank. 'No one will take control of Saint Domingue without the aid of Toussaint l'Ouverture.'

'Two Song who?' Grey demanded.

'Toussaint l'Ouverture, sir, the leader of the rebels.'

'Hm, that's what he calls himself, is it? A black, ain't he?'

'Yes, sir, and a very remarkable one at that.'

The general sniffed. 'How many men under his command?'

'From what I could tell, something between five and ten thousand.'

'All blacks?'

'Blacks, mulattos and French National Guardsmen. He has some high-ranking Spanish military advisers but not, I think, many troops from the neighbouring colony.'

'Artillery?'

'None that I could see.' Keene observed Grey's smile. 'But he don't need it with the kind of war he's waging.'

'Expert on the art of war, are you?' Jervis enquired with the suggestion of a smirk.

Keene outstared the admiral. 'No, sir, but I have my wits about me, I thank God. No intelligent commander would encumber himself with cannon in the forested hills of Saint Domingue.'

Grey tried another tack. 'Where does this fellow's loyalty lie? As I understand the slave revolt is against the French – royalists, Revolutionaries, the lot. So, is he ready for some kind of a deal? He could be very useful to us as a diversion while we secure the main towns and ports.'

Keene looked at the two men before him and saw the closed corporate mind of the establishment. Was there any point in trying to enlighten them? Whatever he said they would almost certainly throw British soldiers and seamen into the French islands, trusting implicitly in the natural superiority of their military system, irrespective of the realities facing them on the ground. Yet, automatically, Keene found himself uttering what was in his mind. 'I think, sir, you'd find Toussaint too sophisticated to let himself be used as a pawn in any political manoeuvre.'

At that the two older men glanced at each other and burst into laughter. Grey said, 'M'dear Keene, the fellow's a savage! Challoner told me you were aptly named – "Keene name, keen mind", he said. I reckon you've been a bit too long in the tropics. Too much sun gives men odd ideas.'

Keene shrugged. 'You gentlemen asked for information. I tell you as simply as I can what I know. What you choose to do – or not do – with it is a matter for your own judgement – and your own consciences. You ask where Toussaint l'Ouverture's loyalty lies. In my opinion he is committed above all else to his own people. He will be the friend of any nation who genuinely helps him to achieve liberty for the slaves. And the implacable enemy of anyone who tries to stop him achieving that objective. In that regard he is a man in the same mould as George Washington, and his Majesty's government would do well to consider whether they handled that gentleman as wisely as they might.'

Keene felt Hawkestone stiffen beside him with embarrassment and anxiety.

Jervis's face reddened and he glowered across the cabin. 'Do you realise, young man, that you're in the presence of an officer who was decorated for bravery in the war against the American rebels and appointed commander-in-chief of British forces in the latter stages of that war?'

Grey waved the comment aside. 'Enough of that, John. I like a man who speaks his mind.'

Jervis was not to be mollified. 'You may say so, but I've had men under my command flogged for such impertinence.'

Keene remarked languidly, 'Then, sir, what a mercy – for both of us – that I ain't under your command.'

When, minutes later, they were being rowed back to the *Promise* Hawkestone maintained an austere silence. Only in the privacy of his cabin did the captain release his pent-up fury. 'What the devil d'ye mean by that, George! You've just made an enemy of two very powerful men.'

Keene shrugged. 'Two powerful, old, stupid men!'

'It may not matter to you but Jervis can hamper my career – has probably already decided to do so!'

'If your career depends on men like that I pity you!'

'Well, it does – and I'm damned if I want your pity!' Hawkestone was now leaning on the chart table, knuckles of his clenched fists white against the polished wood. 'We can't all be free spirits like George Keene, going where we will and be damned to anyone who gets in the way!'

Keene's temper was slipping from his control. 'You charge me with trampling on other men's feelings? That's remarkably drole coming from the so-called "friend" who stole away the woman I loved!'

The words obviously stung and as soon as Keene had uttered them he wished them unsaid. For several seconds Hawkestone stared speechless across the table. Then he shouted, 'Get out! Get out or, by God, I'll have you thrown in the brig.'

Over the next few days the two men avoided each other as far as was possible within the close confines of a ship 130 feet long by 35 feet wide. When they spoke it was with the utmost economy of words. Both men regretted what had passed between them. Neither was ready to take the initiative in putting things right.

Five days of dispiriting inactivity came to an end when Hawkestone was once more summoned aboard the flagship. Jervis had called a conference of captains and the *Promise*'s commander was visibly pleased and relieved to be included in their number. When he returned from the *Boyne* he ordered his officers to attend him in the great cabin. Keene joined the assembly half expecting to be dismissed but Hawkestone was too taken up with the importance of the news he had to impart to pay any attention to the presence of a civilian. He seated himself at the table and surveyed the dozen young men who stood opposite, casting apprehensive glances at one another.

'Gentlemen,' Hawkestone said, 'I have good news. We

are to see action, at last. We sail in the morning for Martinique to intercept a French squadron reported heading for Fort Royal. Now we can show the fleet what the old *Promise* can do.'

There were murmurs of approval and as Keene looked round at the others there could be no doubt that, to a man, they were delighted at the prospect of getting to grips with the enemy and the possibility of earning prize money. Hawkestone explained in more detail the orders he had received from the admiral. Fort Royal was France's principal naval port and arsenal in the West Indies. Intelligence reports indicated that there were few warships in the harbour and that the garrison was severely undermanned. However, news of the Jervis-Grey expedition had spurred Paris into sending reinforcements and a squadron was expected to arrive within the week. Jervis had detailed seven ships to engage the enemy vessels and prevent them reaching their destination.

Keene hung back when the others departed. From the doorway, he said in a tone that he tried not to make critical, 'I thought you were under Challoner's orders to head back directly to England once you had made your report to Jervis.'

Hawkestone was busying himself with charts and did not look up as he said, 'Well, Jervis is here and Sir Thomas ain't.'

Keene shrugged and turned but stopped when Hawkestone continued, 'The admiral's given me a chance to get back into his good graces. He knows the *Promise* ain't under his command but he's offered an opportunity for action at Martinique, as he says to prove I'm a "loyal navy man". I can't afford to turn my back on it.'

'Well, I hope Challoner don't mind being kept waiting.'

'Challoner be damned! And you're the last man to lecture me about devotion to Challoner. You've turned your back on him for good and all. Well, like you, I don't intend to let the little grey fox ruin my life. Besides, if I sailed the

161

Promise away from here now I'd probably have a mutiny on my hands. The crew don't relish the thought of being jeered at by other ships' companies. It's been bad enough these past months deliberately avoiding any chance of action. If we made for home now, while Jervis's fleet is poised to take over the French West Indies, I'd have the devil's own job keeping control of the men.'

'I see. Then I'll leave you to your plans.' Keene put a hand to the door latch.

'One more thing, George,' Hawkestone called out.

'Yes.'

'The admiral invites you to have supper with him. In private. Seven sharp.'

Fourteen

Jervis's private dining cabin, to which Keene was escorted that evening, was a small room on the larboard side of the stern. A large part of it was taken up by the carriages of two cannon and the remaining space was just sufficient for a table and five chairs. However, since Keene was the admiral's only guest, the atmosphere was not claustrophobic.

'We need total secrecy for this meeting,' Jervis explained. He sat at one end of the table, his left hand resting on the head of a black mastiff whose eyes, dark with suspicion, regarded his master's companion with ill-concealed hostility. When Keene returned no comment, he went on, 'I suppose you are puzzled by my invitation.'

Keene's reply was cautious. 'One needs to know a man well to be surprised by anything he does.'

'Then be prepared to learn.' The admiral gazed across the table with frank, unsmiling eyes. *'Que pensez-vous de la situation à Paris? Le petit dandy, Robespierre, il a le pouvoir absolu? Peut-être il y a des rivals potentiels?'*

Keene listened to the precise, bookish French delivered with little trace of an authentic accent. He replied in the same language that, yes, as far as he could tell, Robespierre was, indeed, in command. As to any threat to his position from rivals, in politics, particularly radical politics, there were always 'colleagues' watching for an opportunity to displace the leader.

Jervis reverted to his native tongue. 'Self-taught. Never had much in the way of proper schooling. Took three years out in the seventies to travel around Europe and learn other languages. French has been very useful since we've gone back to war with the Frogs – interrogating prisoners, and that sort of thing. I suppose you had private tutors and a wealthy father to send you off on the grand tour.'

Keene provided the curtest of answers. 'My father was a farm labourer. Such education as I've received was courtesy of the Marquis of Stafford and his son, Lord Gower, my patron. Like you, sir, I picked up languages on the hoof around Europe.'

'Really, young man? Well, well, I took you for a gentleman born – you have the bearing and the arrogance.'

There seemed no answer to that and Keene remained silent. The mastiff slumped down, having finally accepted the stranger's presence. Jervis's servant set food on the table. Conversation drifted awkwardly, like uncertain currents in a sluggish stream, until the admiral announced portentously, 'Intelligence.'

Keene looked up quizzically.

'Intelligence, spying, information gathering, call it what you like – you and I know the importance of it.'

Keene nodded cautiously and tried to decide what it was the older man seemed to be having difficulty in saying.

'There are men of rank in the navy, and in the army – Grey's one of 'em – who don't see the value of it. Well, I do. That's why I've great respect for your director, Challoner.'

'I didn't realise you knew Sir Thomas.'

'I've never met him. Don't know many people who have. But his name's a legend. Evan Nepean calls him simply the "master". You've met Nepean, of course.'

Keene nodded. Nepean was officially a secretary at the Home Office. His real function was intelligence adviser to Henry Dundas, William Pitt's bosom companion and closest supporter in the Commons. More importantly from Keene's point of view, the Prime Minister used Dundas to coordinate covert information which came from a variety of sources in order to provide a basis for well-founded government decisions. Dundas and Challoner worked closely together, though from odd comments Sir Thomas had made Keene gathered that he did not altogether trust the man he referred to as an 'uncouth Scot'.

Jervis might have been reading Keene's thoughts. He said, 'Nepean is Dundas's whipping boy and my friends in the Admiralty tell me that Dundas wants to have the running of this war. Among the many profitable offices he holds is the treasurership of the navy. He uses the power that gives him to try to control old Philip Stephens, who's been secretary to the Admiralty for about thirty years. You can't possibly realise just what that means. Stephens *is* the Admiralty. Everything goes through his hands – and damned competent hands they are too. He controls the flow of intelligence, collects information from ships' captains all over the world and deploys his own agents. We've all come to trust him. He's a navy man through and through. He understands warfare at sea. Better still, he understands seamen. He stands between us and the politicians; maintains a degree of independence for the Admiralty. It's no secret that Dundas wants to elbow him aside and put Nepean in his place.'

'Nepean's a good man,' Keene suggested.

The admiral nodded solemnly. 'None better – for a landsman.'

At last Keene began to see the harbour towards which this serpentine conversational voyage was headed. 'I imagine you'd like to see Dundas's plans frustrated,' he ventured.

Jervis sat back in his chair and rang a hand bell. The servant immediately reappeared to clear the table and set upon it a ship's decanter and glasses. When they were alone again Jervis pushed the vessel towards Keene and he poured himself a measure of brandy.

The admiral approached obliquely his answer to the question. 'There's a lot of captains who'd be circumspect about passing information direct to Dundas. They wouldn't trust him to give it due weight. They'd suspect him of putting his own gloss on it.'

'That could lead to the suppression of vital intelligence.'

'Precisely!' Jervis thumped the table so heavily with his fist that the glasses jumped. 'Now you and I, young man, see that danger very clearly. Therefore, it's our responsibility to do something about it.'

Keene took a mouthful of the excellent spirit and savoured it while he pondered his response. 'What have you in mind?' he asked.

'I want you to be a direct link from me to Challoner.'

Keene groaned inwardly. It was this kind of personality politics which was making it difficult to run an efficient intelligence service. Every man with foreign contacts aspired to be his own spymaster. Diplomats, officers, merchants, politicians, aristocratic travellers, hot-headed royalist enthusiasts – all believed themselves possessed of vital information and valued contacts, all wanted access to government and court circles, all regarded other intelligence gatherers as rivals rather than colleagues united in a common cause. Such 'amateurs' were the bane of Challoner's life. Fortunately, this instance of clandestine activity was destined to go no further. Keene had no intention of reporting back to Challoner. In fact, he was already making plans to use the forthcoming naval engagement in which the *Promise* would be involved as a means of engineering his disappearance. There was, therefore, no reason not to encourage Jervis's scheming. 'I couldn't undertake that on my own authority,' he said.

'Of course not, but you can take back with you certain letters I've written for Challoner and you can report to him the substance of this conversation.'

Keene drank more cognac. 'That presupposes my safe return to England,' he observed.

'What the devil d'ye mean by that?'

'You've ordered the *Promise* into battle. Anything could happen to the ship or me.'

Jervis came his closest to a laugh. 'You need have no concern on that score. *Promise* is only going on the interception squadron because young Hawkestone begged for action.'

'He asked *you* for a position?'

The admiral nodded. 'After our little disagreement the other day he sent a message assuring me of his personal loyalty and asking for an opportunity to display it. Unnecessary, of course. I thought no ill of the lad. He comes of good naval stock. But he needs an opportunity to prove something to himself. So, he sails for Martinique tomorrow. But he'll come to no harm. Captain Granger of the *Sentinel* is in charge and he has orders to keep the *Promise* out of the thick of the action and to send her on her way to England at the first opportunity. With God's grace and fair winds you'll be home before February is out.' He poured himself more brandy. 'Of course, all this is strictly between ourselves. Not a breath of it to Hawkestone – on your word, now.'

'You have my assurance of that.' Keene looked at the old man and reassessed his opinion. Jervis was no fool whose attitudes had been moulded by traditions uncritically accepted. Behind the uniform there was a man of lively mind and independent judgement – a difficult man to like, perhaps, but an easy one to respect.

Jervis kept his visitor aboard the flagship till late. He seemed to enjoy the company of a young companion who was not under his command and who did not, therefore, have to weigh carefully every word he spoke. When, finally, Keene climbed unsteadily aboard the *Promise* he found Hawkestone anxiously awaiting his return. What did the admiral want, he asked as Keene made his way to his cabin with one hand clapped to his throbbing forehead. What could they possibly have found to discuss all this time? Was Jervis quizzing Keene about him?

Keene lay down on his cot, giving monosyllabic answers to questions. Those questions were still coming thick and fast when he slipped into unconsciousness.

Derek Wilson

By the time he awoke the next morning the *Promise* was already under way. Keene did not hurry over his toilet and the sun was well up before he joined Hawkestone on the quarterdeck. Immediately the inquisition was resumed but now Keene was able to give the young captain the reassurance he craved. 'Jervis thinks very highly of you. He believes you have the makings of a first-rate commander.'

'Truly?' Hawkestone asked.

'Truly,' Keene said. 'This is the life you were made for.' He looked across the water at the six other vessels making a proud show as they creamed across the waves before a following wind. The seventy-four-gun *Sentinel* led the column of three line-of-battle ships and four frigates and Keene could understand how a young captain might see in that picture an image of his own career prospects. He said, 'I've had plenty of opportunity to watch how you handle a warship and her crew – not to mention how you handle yourself. If Britain has enough captains of your calibre this war will be a short one. I said as much to Jervis.'

'That was uncommonly generous of you, Charles – after what passed between us recently.'

Keene waved a hand. 'Forgotten. Oh, and for what it's worth, I was wrong about Jervis.'

It was four days later, towards the end of the afternoon, that a lookout in the *Sentinel*'s foretop had a first sight of the enemy. Every captain in the convoy sent his keenest-eyed ratings aloft to observe details about the size and quality of the French force. By the time the light faded fifteen sail had been identified and they were seen to alter course to the north-west to avoid an engagement.

Granger, carrying the temporary rank of commodore, ordered his ships to follow and close with the enemy at maximum speed. However, as dawn light crept across the ocean the next day the circle of the horizon was unbroken.

Hawkestone snapped his telescope shut and stamped

168

about the quarterdeck. 'Cowardly Frogs,' he muttered. 'I'll wager they've dispersed under cover of darkness.'

'Dispersed?' Keene asked. 'Why would they do that? Surely their admiral would want to keep all his fleet together if he thought there was the prospect of a battle. He must know he has the advantage of numbers.'

Hawkestone smiled grimly, gaining some satisfaction from explaining naval tactics to a novice. 'He knows we'll have to divide our force in an effort to locate him. That means that some of his fleet will almost certainly escape and that any ships which do fall in with some of ours will have more than even odds.'

His assessment of the situation was immediately confirmed. The *Sentinel* took in sail and a flag signal sent to the squadron summoned all captains aboard for an urgent conference. It was brief and when Hawkestone returned from the flagship he was in an evil mood. For several minutes he busied himself giving instructions about sail settings and helmsman's course. Then he descended to his cabin, where Keene joined him.

He found the captain staring moodily out of the stern window at the other ships which were dispersing in pairs. 'What's the matter, Charles?' Keene asked.

Hawkestone did not turn. 'Sent packing!' he muttered. 'Like children pushed out of the way when their parents are too busy for 'em.'

Keene waited for his friend to explain.

Hawkestone slumped into his heavy armchair. 'Captain Granger is dividing the squadron to go in search of the enemy. But the *Promise*, because she carries important despatches for London – God rot Challoner! – is dismissed.'

Keene went to a small chest in the corner of the cabin. As he took out a bottle and a pair of horn beakers the lid slammed down. 'Feels like a squall,' he observed as he brought the rum carefully to the table. 'Let's drink to a safe voyage and damnation to the Frogs.'

The landsman's efforts to cheer Hawkestone were not very successful but the captain soon had other things to occupy his mind. The storm whose first blast Keene had felt came on with speed and ferocity. Officers and crew were suddenly busy taking in sail, closing ports, stowing and battening down anything that could roll around the decks causing damage or injury. Keene stayed in his cabin out of their way. When he did venture out, clinging to rail or rope to avoid crashing to the slippery, heaving deck, there was nothing to see. Rain and spray made an opaque screen which blocked out the whole world beyond some fifty yards from the frigate.

Then, as quickly as it had arrived, the storm moved on. Shafts of sunlight gleamed the sodden spars and sparkled the droplets of water that spattered down to the deck. Keene watched the backside of the tempest as it rolled across the water, like a curtain being pulled back to reveal a painted theatrical seascape.

It revealed something else. There, not a mile away on the starboard bow, four French ships lay scattered over half a mile of ocean.

'Sail!' Keene yelled and half a dozen other voices echoed the cry from sailors who had also seen the enemy ships.

Hawkestone rushed to the bow rail, wiping the lens of his spyglass as he came. 'Three large third-raters and a frigate,' he said as Keene joined him. 'One of the bigger ships is damaged – lost some top timber. That'll slow 'em down.'

'We'd better go about and find some of our squadron,' Keene suggested.

Hawkestone made no reply, staring intently at the enemy ships. 'She's stuck,' he muttered. 'Cornered.' Then, more excitedly, 'By God, it's their flagship! The others won't dare leave her! If we could get in close and do some more damage . . .'

'Charles! One against four? Those are damnably poor odds.'

Still the captain stood, gazing at the enemy like one transfixed.

Keene grabbed him by the arm. 'Heroic, Charles, but bad tactics. If the *Promise* gets blown out of the water those Frenchies will get clear away. Give their position to our squadron and they'll almost certainly be caught.'

With a long sigh Hawkestone turned to the watch officer. 'Mr Cutt, turn her about, if you please. Come below and I'll give you your new course.'

Keene idled at the bow rail as the frigate came round into the wind. On deck and aloft there was a state of what would have appeared to a layman as confusion as men scurried about in obedience to the shrill signals of the bosun's call and the shouted orders of his mates. Keene knew how hard their task was, how precisely the sails had to be set so that the ship could make way against the vestigial blasts of the storm.

He had his own problems to think about which involved just as nice a calculation. Time was running short for the staging of his disappearance. The *Promise* would make a couple of landfalls on her way back to England, for essential revictualling. At one of these ports of call he would have to stage a fatal 'accident', seen by sufficient members of the crew to convince any Challoner inquest.

A shower of spray swept over him and he moved swiftly away from the rail. He strode the length of the bouncing ship deep in thought. It was as he was climbing to the quarterdeck that he heard a cry from aloft, 'A sail! A sail!' 'Whither away?' came the response from the midshipman at the helm. 'Dead astern!'

Crossing to the stern rail, Keene stared out across the widening expanse of water between *Promise* and the French ships. He saw one of the frigates detaching itself from its fellows to give chase to the English vessel.

Moments later Hawkestone joined him. He smiled grimly. 'They know what we're about and want to stop us reporting their position to our fleet.'

'We can outrun the Frog, can't we?'

'Probably – if we want to.' Hawkestone looked thought-ful.

Keene frowned. 'More heroics, Charles. Just because the odds have evened . . . '

There was a gleam in the captain's eye as he replied. 'No, I'm not thinking of a flamboyant gesture – leastways, not entirely. You were right about the importance of tactics. Now, we could race yon Frog for an hour or two, however long it takes to find some of the squadron. What would her captain do then?'

'Turn tail?'

'Sure to, by my reckoning. He'll have no stomach for an unequal fight. But if we can bring him to an action before he gets nervous, our friends will hear the gunfire and come running.'

'So will the Frogs.'

'So much the better. We can settle scores with several of the enemy at one go.'

'And *Promise* will be in the thick of it?'

Hawkestone smiled. '*Promise* will have obeyed orders and used initiative – hardly court martial offences.'

Keene read the excitement and deep satisfaction in his friend's eyes. Everything had fallen into place for him. He was about to take part in the major engagement he craved and, as he said, he could do so without 'stretching' the interpretation of his orders. Keene hoped that all would turn out well for him and his crew. He reflected that the forthcoming action might somehow serve his own purpose. It should be possible to find a way to go missing in the heat of battle. Why, then, he asked himself, did he have a sense of foreboding?

Fifteen

The chase lasted a little more than two hours. The two frigates were well matched and if Hawkestone had not occasionally deliberately allowed the sails to get out of trim, the *Promise* would have had little difficulty outrunning her pursuer. He used the time to make leisurely and careful preparations. All hands were piped to battle stations and the cannon unlashed and run out. The decks were cleared, powder and linstocks brought up from the magazine, and small arms distributed.

Slowly the French frigate closed the distance. Aboard the *Promise* all was tense expectation. From the main deck eyes were turned toward the captain, all ears listening for those orders which would signal the start of battle. Hawkestone maintained his course. He had topmen watching forrard for the first sighting of British ships and others gauging the progress of the enemy.

The Frenchie, later identified as the *Éclair*, opened hostilities when she still lay more than a thousand yards astern. Repeated shots from her bow chaser fell well short.

Hawkestone laughed. 'Let him waste his powder!' Keene saw that the young captain was flushed with excitement and anticipation, emotions he shared, though for other reasons.

Hawkestone turned to the officer beside him and gave his instructions crisply. 'Look at her course. She intends to come up with us on our larboard side and give us the benefit of her starboard cannon. Good! Good! Mr Cutt, close me the larboard ports. I'll have extra men to the helm and sail crews on their toes. When I give the order "Come about to larboard" I want to see the fastest hundred and eighty degree turn you've ever done in your life.'

'Ay, ay, sir,' the lieutenant solemnly responded, and immediately bellowed a string of orders to the main deck.

Seconds later a cry came from the foretop, 'Sail ho!'

All eyes on the quarterdeck turned to scan the horizon ahead but nothing could be seen from that level. Cutt demanded details from the watch and received the reply, 'Two ships fine on the larboard bow.'

Hawkestone muttered, 'They must be ours.'

'Could be part of the French fleet,' Keene suggested.

'We'll have to take a chance on that,' the captain replied. 'Mr Cutt, come about to larboard, if you please.'

The frigate exploded into what seemed chaotic action as teams of men hauled on ropes and hastened to make them fast. Spars creaked in response. Sails flapped. *Promise* heeled steeply to the left, her gunwale almost level with the waves. Keene braced himself as the ship completed the manoeuvre. The sails adjusted to their new trim and bellied out.

'Open larboard ports and run out guns,' Hawkestone ordered. 'Now, let's see what yon Frenchie's made of that.' He bounded down the companionway and along the main deck to stand by the forward rail, telescope raised to his eye.

Keene joined him at a more leisurely pace. He found the captain jubilant. Hawkestone chuckled, handing the glass to Keene. 'That's set 'em all at sixes and sevens!'

Keene trained the telescope on the vessel with which they were now rapidly closing. The Frenchman was feverishly taking in sail. On her deck gun crews were hauling in the starboard cannon and falling over themselves to run out the guns on the other side.

'Let's give 'em some encouragement. Bow gun,' Hawkestone ordered, 'fire at will!'

The six-pounder in the forecastle immediately coughed out its challenge and kept up a barrage a fast as its crew could reload.

The two ships were now coming abreast of each other with little more than a hundred yards of open sea between them. Hawkestone returned to the quarterdeck but Keene, having found an observation point where he was least in the way, remained close to the bowsprit to survey the action.

Promise got her twelve-pounder shots in first almost unopposed. As her larboard guns fired in order on the initial pass their crews quickly found the right elevation. The first shots passed across the enemy at mainsail height, one taking away part of the *Éclair*'s foremast rigging. Subsequent balls found the frigate's main and gun decks. Between the roar of the cannon Keene could hear the screams of injured Frenchmen. Only two of the *Éclair*'s sternmost guns made reply before *Promise* had passed.

Now the British ship made another turn to come round behind the enemy and strike at her starboard side. The manoeuvre took several minutes and Keene watched closely how the time was filled. The captain ordered a boarding party to be ready, armed with axes, pistols and cutlasses. He stationed men with grappling lines at bow and stern and sent aloft others armed with muskets. He ordered the main deck guns to load with grapeshot to wreak maximum havoc among the foreign crew. The *Promise* was set on a course which would bring her within grappling range and crewmen stood ready to take in sail. It was obvious that Hawkestone was set on a sudden decisive strike at the enemy vessel rather than a prolonged bombardment aimed at battering her into submission. It was the riskier of the available options but the reason was not difficult to see: the British captain and crew were intent on taking a prize and doing so before any other British vessel appeared to share the action and the proceeds.

Keene now made his move. Hurrying to the quarterdeck, he strode up to the captain. 'Charles,' he said. 'I'd like to join the boarding party.'

Hawkestone was busy giving orders and watching the progress of the battle. He had only time for a brief glance at his friend. 'Very well,' he said. Then, to Cutt, 'Larboard guns commence firing.'

The roar of *Promise*'s twelve-pounders rocked the frigate as Keene stepped to the companionway. He missed his footing and went sprawling to the deck.

This time there was no question of the *Éclair* being caught unawares. Her armament opened up in thunderous response. Keene heard the crunch of smashed timber close to his head and felt the wind of the roundshot as it passed by him. He lifted his eyes to see a gaping hole in the side planking not two yards away. Behind him he heard the screams of injured men. He scrambled to his feet and almost fell again on a deck slippery with blood.

The quarterdeck was chaos. Men and timber fragments lay sprawled and jumbled together in a red pool that gushed from shattered limbs and spread rapidly over the sanded boards. Keene staggered across to give what help he could. From among the human wreckage at the foot of the mizzenmast Lieutenant Cutt emerged. He was on his knees and shaking his head, one hand clutching a scarlet-soaked shoulder of his uniform jacket. 'The captain,' he muttered dazedly.

Keene looked down. Charles Hawkestone lay on his back, head at a sharp angle, eyes wide open, lips curved into what looked like a smile. The entire front of his coat and shirt were torn open by the savage splinters which had ripped through to the bone.

An anger such as he had never felt before welled up inside Keene. 'Are you fit to take over, Cutt?' he demanded.

The lieutenant nodded.

'Good, then let's make those Frog bastards pay for this!'

He leaped down to the main deck, stooped to grab a cutlass that had fallen from the hand of a dead sailor, and ran to the rail waving it wildly and shouting every French imprecation that came into his head. Around, smoke and spray swirled. Beneath his feet, *Promise* bucked and reared with the force of shots delivered and received. He was oblivious to it all and careless of danger. His attention remained fixed on the deck of the French frigate which came slowly closer, grappled now by the ropes and hooks hurled from its adversary.

At last, with savage shrieks, the British boarders swung across the gap. The first wave landed and engaged the enemy hand-to-hand. Keene caught a swinging rope and leaped out over the water. 'As good a way as any to die,' he thought.

Epilogue

Homecoming – 16 March 1794

I t was, Keene reflected, a year to the day since he had been 'volunteered' for membership of Sir Thomas Challoner's foreign service. The images were vivid in his mind – the explosion which sundered the transport ship *Spry* into a million pieces scattered over the surface of the Atlantic, his 'rescue' and clandestine conveyance to a secluded country house, his meeting with the sardonic grey 'fox' who was determined to dominate his life, try as Keene might to take that life back into his own hands. A year? Dear God, it seemed like an age, an entire existence. So many dangers, so many tragedies, so many sorrows had crammed themselves into those twelve months. So many triumphs? Keene did not know. His masters might attach that word to missions successfully accomplished. All he could think of was the dead – Charlotte Corday, Paul Vivier, Charles Hawkestone, and others who did not deserve the violence which had torn them from the ranks of the living. And for what? That question too hung in the vacant spaces of his mind, vainly seeking an answer. There had been times on the homeward voyage when he had been convinced that he was losing his mind. Demons of grief and anger and guilt assailed his waking and most of his sleeping moments. They inveighed against the creatures safe in their London, Paris and Philadelphia houses who sent others to dirty or bloody their hands. They cried out against a God who could allow lovely, pure, honourable people to be the victims of cynical

178

elites. But most of all they waved their accusing arms at George Keene, who had had the effrontery to survive while his betters were destroyed. Reason's voice was drowned by the banshee wailing of his inner ghosts. Of one thing only could George Keene be absolutely certain as he watched the Kent coast slipping quietly by on this calm March morning: he was not the same man who had left the shores of Britain those long months ago.

He had come unscathed through the fighting aboard the *Éclair*, not because he had taken care to defend himself, but quite the reverse. He had flailed about him with the abandoned fury of an avenging angel, seeing but dimly, through a red haze, the French sailors who went down before him or fled his dripping cutlass. At the last it was two of the *Promise*'s crewmen who had had to restrain him. They told him that the battle was over; that the Frog captain had struck his colours. He had returned to the British frigate in a daze and it was only later that he learned from the conversation of men whose memories were clearer than his own that the fight for the *Éclair* had been disappointingly brief. The French ship had been desperately undermanned and had put up little resistance once she had been boarded. It was the easy victory that Hawkestone's crew had long hoped for. But there was no rejoicing aboard the *Promise*.

There was just the solemn, dispiriting work of clearing up. Groups of men washed blood from the decks. The ship's carpenter made good the damage the *Promise* had suffered. The surgeon and his team did their limited best to save the injured. And the frigate's complement buried their dead. Four bodies were committed to the deep at the dawn following the battle. George looked down at the meaningless, identical bundles lying on the deck, stitched into their sailcloth shrouds. There was nothing to distinguish Charles Hawkestone from the three able seamen who had given their lives in the same cause.

After the ceremony, Sam Cutt, his left arm in a sling, came to stand beside Keene at the aft rail. They both stared at the wake stretching out behind *Promise* to the point where Hawkestone had entered the water.

'He would have been a great leader,' the lieutenant said.

'He was,' Keene responded.

Cutt nodded. Never a man of words, he was at this solemn moment totally bereft. After a long silence he said. 'There are the captain's papers and things to be sorted out for his widow . . .' He faltered. 'When we get back to Barbados, Jervis will, as like as not, give us a new captain . . . He'll want the great cabin . . . I thought you, being Captain Hawkestone's friend . . .'

Keene sighed. 'Yes, Sam, I'll look after everything . . . Later.'

When he steeled himself to the task that afternoon he found that there was, in fact, little to be done. Charles's clothes were neatly folded in their chest, with his Bible, letters, four books and some trinkets. There were a few pieces of crested silver, a writing box and the necessary brushes and shaving gear. Post-captains usually travelled light and Hawkestone had been more than usually frugal about surrounding himself with possessions. The most poignant was a gold locket the surgeon had removed from around Charles's neck. Keene opened it and saw Thérèse's dark eyes looking into his own. Quickly he snapped it shut again.

Hawkestone's log and papers were all in order in the cupboard below the chart table. There was a long, detailed report for Challoner as well as letters to Thérèse and to Charles's father, ready for posting as soon as *Promise* reached home waters. There was also a large, sealed item addressed, 'To my very good friend George Keene Esquire'.

For several minutes Keene sat in the captain's chair, the letter lying before him on the table unopened. When at last he could bring himself to break the seal and smooth out the heavy paper, he read:

> My dear George, I feel rather absurd writing something that, please God, you will never read. But if

you do there are important matters to be settled and I will only rest easy in the knowledge that you will humour me by taking good care to arrange things as they should be arranged. Dammit, how pompous this do read.

George, you know that Thérèse and Georgie are the dearest things in this world to me. You know it because you feel the same yourself. You can't imagine what a comfort that is to me. You will care for them as I would have done. Probably better – you ain't got salt water in your veins. If you have any regard for me this is what you will do for me and for all of us and now there can't be no arguing about it.

Go to Collingbourne. Give Thérèse the letter enclosed with this. It will tell her that it is my dearest wish that you and she should wed and find happiness together wherever in the world you should both have to go in search of it. Arrangements have been made with the family solicitor for a settlement on Thérèse which will be sufficient for you to find a new life somewhere. As for little Georgie, Collingbourne will one day be his and it's my hope that, when this wretched war is over, he and his mother and you will be able to return there. Bring up the lad to be a good English gentleman, George. I can think of no better tutor for him. Impress upon Thérèse that she should not hesitate for a single day to follow her heart in this matter. No need to go through the respectable proprieties of a long mourning. It is *absolutely* my wish that she should go with you if she feels for you as I know she does.

And so, farewell my dear friend. Try ever to think well of him who sometime behaved knavishly towards you but ever held you in the very highest esteem, your true friend,

Charles Hawkestone

Admiral Jervis had added another to Keene's list of commissions – personal letters to Hawkestone's father and widow. He had transferred to the *Promise* Captain John Craig, a middle-aged, unimaginative career officer, and, as soon as she could be made ready for the ocean crossing, he had ordered her back to England. Back in the Channel after an uneventful voyage, Keene had sent the admiral's messages to Collingbourne via a Weymouth fishing boat while the *Promise* had continued towards the Thames estuary.

Now she was in the Medway, on the last stage of her journey to Chatham dockyard. Most of the seamen had packed their chests in readiness for going ashore. There was aboard all the excitement associated with homecoming. Sailors not employed on specific duties lined the rails, looking out across the sandbanks and the flat landscape, their minds on the roads that led to distant towns and villages, or, perhaps, simply on the Chatham stews.

Keene could not share their eager anticipation. Nor could he analyse his feelings. He simply nursed an iron determination. Amidst all the chaos of war, the waste of shattered lives, the political confusion of men and nations, there was only one thing that he, George Keene, could accomplish. Whether his exploits in the service of Mr Pitt's spymaster had made one iota of difference to the fate of men or nations, he could not say. Whether information he had gathered would shorten the war or save lives or deflect his Majesty's government from any of its more disastrous policies, other minds than his would have to decide. But he held in his hands the fate of three people and he felt deeply the trust of others who had believed in him. Now he knew that it was not fanciful to see these two as intertwined. To make a future for himself, for the woman he loved and for their son was to affirm a belief in humanity; to make a statement that individuals, and therefore nations, could survive the machinations of politicians, the rivalries of classes and the clashes of ideals. As soon as *Promise* dropped anchor he would go ashore and take carriage for Wiltshire, avoiding

London. Non-stop driving would bring him within hours to Collingbourne. Then, if Thérèse was ready, they could make an immediate start on their new life.

Shortly before noon the *Promise* came to anchor in the outer roadstead of Chatham dockyard. She was just one among a host of naval vessels gathered in the Admiralty's great dockyard. However, as the latest arrival she was soon the centre of attraction for a flotilla of small boats – traders seeking to sell local produce, buy foreign trinkets from homecoming mariners, or ferry paying passengers to the shore.

Keene surveyed the scurrying craft and listened to the shouts of hawkers offering their wares or services. He was on the lookout for a sturdy boat capable of carrying himself and Hawkestone's chest. He opened Charles's telescope for a clearer view of the approaching vessels. Some were bringing visitors across the anchorage – the wives and children of returning sailors. He passed over one boat with a couple seated in its stern. Then, with a gasp, he brought the spyglass to bear once more.

Was it . . . ? Yes it was – Thérèse! Sombrely dressed, as befitted a widow, but beautiful, oh so beautiful. Keene's pulse raced. Then he focused on the figure beside her, hands clasped over the handle of his cane. Sir Thomas Challoner!